WHY DOES HE DO IT?

"For arson, we get motives galore. Insurance is the biggest one, of course. Then there's revenge—discharged employee burning down the plant because he's mad at the boss. There's jealousy, too, and sometimes fire as a cover-up for murder. Lots of motives like that. Not all of them seem completely sane or rational reasons, but we can understand them. It's the other kind we're afraid of. The cases where there is no motive, no sense. The torch doesn't have a reason for setting fires—at least, not one he can understand. Voices tell him to do it, or he likes to see things burn, or he wants to watch the firemen come and maybe even run into the flames himself and be a hero. Many times a firebug doesn't even seem to realize what he's done—it's as though the whole experience was blotted out of his consciousness."

ROBERT BLOCH

FIREBUG

A TOM DOHERTY ASSOCIATES BOOK
NEW YORK

This is a work of fiction in a fictional setting. Any resemblance to persons living or dead is purely coincidental and would scare the author half to death.

FIREBUG

Copyright © 1961 by Robert Bloch

A TOR Book
Published by Tom Doherty Associates, Inc.
49 West 24 Street
New York, N.Y. 10010

Cover art by Jim Warren

ISBN: 0-812-51578-1   Can. ISBN: 0-812-51579-X

First Tor edition: October 1988

Printed in the United States of America

0 9 8 7 6 5 4 3 2 1

Dedicated to GORDON MOLSON and Associates—
who lit a fire under me.

0

MY NAME is Philip Dempster; I'm sleeping.

The dream is red. It's always red. Sometimes it's golden-red, like the first flash of a sulphur match. Sometimes it's blue and orange at the edges, like a glow dying away to embers, but it's still red. Red isn't always simply colors— sometimes it's a thing of emotions and the *feeling* of red. It gets to be a *knowing* what's red and what isn't. My dreams are red, always red.

My name is Philip Dempster; I'm dreaming.

In the dream I'm driving my car down a long dark road. Far ahead I see a light. It's the only light in the world, because my car has no headlamps; it's a blind car, and I'm grateful I have eyes, because if I didn't have eyes, then *I'd* be blind in this world, too. And I have

1

to keep looking down the road toward that light . . .

I'm driving and my back hurts. It hurts from leaning over the wheel for so long, staring so hard at that faint trace of light far down the dark road. My eyes burn, as well, but differently. They feel as though they're turning to water, as though I haven't shut them for a long time, as though I've been intentionally keeping them open so they'll burn.

But I know this isn't so. I don't want any part of me to burn.

This must be an illusion.

The dream is real, though. So I keep driving.

The light is getting larger. It's growing much larger, much faster. I apply the brakes and the car begins to slow, but I've deceived myself. I'm no nearer the light. That's strange, for a moment there I thought the light was a flame, and I was about to say: *I'm no nearer the flame.* But it's just a light, I can assure you of that. It's not a flame. It's merely a light . . . you believe me, don't you?

I step on the gas, and the car shoots forward and it isn't as far to the light as I'd supposed. It's just a little way up ahead; in fact, I can see the light is a building, really. It's a bright, glowing building, like a big glowing plastic square sitting in the middle of nowhere. I can't understand why it's out here, but since the long dark road leads back to nowhere, and up ahead, past the building of light, it's nowhere, I know I'll have to stop and ask the way.

My name is Philip Dempster; I'm lost, I think.

I pull off the road and get out of the car. I lock the door behind me. Just one door. The door on the other side is open, unlocked, and it worries me, but I start walking away from the car anyhow. I wish I had locked the other door. It's open, that door. And I know someone could—*what*? What would anyone do? There isn't anyone on the road tonight, so why should I worry? I'm still walking away from the car, and I'm bothered, but I can't turn back now. I have to walk to the building and find out where I am.

That's very important, I think.

The building is on a slight hill, a bit of an incline. I'm walking toward it, and unlike the nearness and farness of the building when I was driving, as I walk it comes much closer, much faster. It almost seems to swallow me. That's a very silly, but a very frightening thought, all at once. I stop walking, because I don't want that building to swallow me.

I stop. But my feet don't stop. They keep walking me up to the building and the building opens its mouth and I see rows and rows of lights that are very toothlike, very sharp and they're waiting waiting, just waiting to swallow me and I tell my feet to *stop Jesus for God's sake stop walking me up to that mouth will you?* But they keep right on walking me up that hill, and now I'm on a bright shining walk, going right into the mouth of the building and I can't tell if I'm large or small or what's really happening except I scream, and it doesn't take. The scream comes out as nothing ... not even a sound. I'm walking fully aware into the mouth of the bright glowing building and now I'm ...

Inside. Far inside the building, and the walls are moist and warm, like a living thing. Could this building *be* alive; could it be a pulsing, breathing thing that needs live flesh to keep it breathing? I hope not.

I'm walking very fast now, and around the bend in the white, moist, pulsing breathing-walls, I can hear someone babbling. It may be talking, but it's a wet, slippery sound, like the bubbling of blood in someone's mouth. I try to hear what's being said, but the words make no sense. It's as if they were being said under water, a great depth, too far away to make any sense.

Then I round the bend and I see the cell. It's a very large cell, and the bars are glowing, translucent, as though lit from within. The bars run up to the white, glowing ceiling, and down into the white, glowing floor. And in the cell is—something—I can't make it out at first—I'm looking—I'm trying to see what it is.

Suddenly I see it clearly. It moves out from behind the bars and I see it. It's a woman. But not really a woman. My throat dries up on me and I try to force my fist into my mouth because I know I'll babble like her if I don't.

The woman is dead.

She's dead. Her limbs are charred, like black-ened branches of a dead tree. But they move. She moves. *It* moves.

It's moving toward the bars now. It shuffles slowly. It's falling to pieces like burned paper, even as I watch it come toward me. My eyes feel as though they'll start from my skull and I try to back up, but I'm rooted to the spot, with the basket in my hands.

The basket? I have a basket don't I? It's filled with something.

The basket is a big basket, and the smell from it is like a hundred incinerators, a thou-sand furnaces where humans have been sent to die, a million grease pits with decaying flesh as their contents. I have the basket in my hands, and as the creature that was a woman bubbles and shambles imbecilically toward me, I pull something from the basket and hurl it at her.

She drops to her knees and begins tearing it with her teeth. She looks up and I see the eyes are black, moist pits of emptiness, the lips are pulled back in a stricture of pain and pleasure, and what hangs from between her teeth, is like spaghetti. But it's not spaghetti. It's a shred of flesh.

Now she beckons me to come closer. I can't help myself. I feel myself being drawn toward her, toward the face that is barely a face any longer, with a vacant pulsing hole where the nose might have been, with the lips cracked and empty of meaning. The spaces so dark and hungry where the sight of her eyes had lain.

She's beckoning to me with a finger that is burned away at the second joint. A stump she crooks at me, and I go toward her.

I don't want to go near her ... she has those deformed, twisted arms extended to me. She's ... she's ... puckering her lips ...

She wants to kiss me!

I scream and my throat tightens at the thought of kissing this corpse, but her arms reach through the bars and encircle me, draw me to her, pull my face up to hers and I see myself staring down into the blackened, ruined abyss of her eye and mouth.

I can't stand it ... I'll go mad ... Help me ... please somebody help me ... save me from this thing, this dead thing ... this thing that keeps murmuring *Save me ... save me ... save me ...*

The lips reach out to me and I'm being swallowed whole by evil and filth and death and the burning of her the heat the burning the insane help the burning I'm burning burning burning I'm

My name is Philip Dempster; my dreams are horrible.

1

BEFORE YOU can have an explosion, somebody must light the fuse.

I was sitting in Tracy's that evening, minding my own business, when Ed Cronin came in. He lit the fuse for me.

The big, heavy-set man took the stool next to mine, but I wasn't aware of him until he nudged my arm.

"Hello, Phil," he said. "How's it going?"

"Down," I told him, lifting my glass.

"The book, I mean."

"Which one?"

"The cult novel."

"Oh, that? So-so, I guess. I'm writing another."

"Glad to hear it," Cronin said.

"I'm not." I signalled to the bartender. "Can't

7

seem to get it organized." The bartender looked at me and I looked at Cronin. "What'll you have?"

He ordered a beer and I took the usual.

"So that's it." Cronin nodded, more to himself than to me. "Some of the boys said you'd been hanging around here lately."

"Bully for them." I raised my glass. "Pretty bright bunch of reporters you've got, Cronin. Always on the lookout for a story. What's your head—PROMISING YOUNG NOVELIST DRINKING HIMSELF TO DEATH?"

Cronin frowned, then put a smile on top of it. "Why not? It's the truth, isn't it?"

"I drink because I like to," I said, and it was a lie. "I'm stuck on the new book, that's all," I said, and it was the truth. "But I can stop drinking whenever I want to." I didn't know whether this was true or false, and it worried me.

"Hate to see you get in the habit." Cronin shrugged. "You're a bright boy, Phil."

"And the way you figure it, bright boys don't drink," I said. "That's where you're wrong. Trying to pin down a personality with a label. In your mind you've got me pegged with that 'bright-boy' tag. Therefore I'm supposed to act thus-and-so. But haven't you ever noticed that people aren't necessarily consistent? They don't run around constantly 'in character' like a bunch of actors playing roles. Sometimes I'm a bright boy, yes. Sometimes I'm a lush, too.

Sometimes I can lick the world, and sometimes I'm scared of my shadow."

Cronin shook his head. "It's not your shadow," he told me. "I've been watching you. Come on, Phil, tell me. What are you afraid of?"

I smiled over at the bartender. "Look, Mac," I said. "Is it all right with you if I climb up and lay down on the bar? My friend here wants to psychoanalyze me."

"Cut it out, Phil. I'm sorry."

"That's all right. But a guy gets mad when somebody asks that kind of question, when all he wants to do is drink in peace—"

"You weren't drinking in peace," Cronin answered. "And I don't think you really want to drink at all."

"Skip it, will you?"

"All right. I didn't mean to go prying into your affairs. That's not why I came over to look for you. Phil, how'd you like to handle an assignment?"

"I'm doing a book."

"But you just said you're hung up on it. And this wouldn't interfere. Only take a few hours a day. Maybe the change of pace would help snap you out of your slump, too."

"What kind of an assignment?"

"Right up your alley. The publisher is going all out on the new Sunday supplement and he's willing to spend a little money. So I sold him the idea of a series of weekly features, say five or six. On local cult rackets."

"That's where I come in, eh?"

"Who else? You're a local boy, you wrote a book about the subject, that makes you an authority."

"Slow down a minute," I told him. "If you're going after the expose angle, you'd better put one of the staff on it—a feature-writer will do you a hatchet-job. I'm not sold on the idea that all cults are rackets. Some of them are legit. I found that out when I was on the Coast, getting material for my book."

Cronin nodded. "I know. And I don't expect you to slant your material. But we've been doing a little checking through the office. We've got a line on five or six outfits here in town that operate in a pretty suspicious manner. These are the ones I want you to work on. And I won't blue-pencil anything unless it's libel. Handle it the way you want—the boss figures it's a public service."

"And if it's lurid enough, it'll help circulation, too," I added.

Cronin shrugged. "Could be. But what do you say? Six features, about fifteen hundred or two thousand words each. We'll let staff follow up on pictures, if we need them. All you have to do is go out, take a look around, then write your story. Shouldn't take more than four-five hours a week."

"What's the price-tag say?"

"The old man was willing to go a hundred and fifty. But I told him your name was worth two hundred. With byline, of course."

Maybe it wasn't all the money in the world,

but I could use twelve hundred dollars for a few hours' work a week. I could very definitely use the money, with my book-royalty check still two months away. A change of pace might snap me out of my slump. It might help me break this habit of sitting and drinking so I could sleep, sleep without dreams, without *the* dream—

"It's a deal," I said. "When do we start?"

"Week from Sunday, if you can deliver," Cronin answered. "Run an announcement in the section this coming Sunday. Today's Monday. Come in and see me tomorrow and I'll line you up with the dope we've got."

"Good enough." I thought it was good, too, because I didn't know he'd just lit the fuse. "How about another drink?"

Cronin slid off the stool. "Sorry, got to be running along. You'll be there in the morning?"

"Sure. Don't worry." I smiled at him. "I'm just staying long enough to have one for the road."

They hadn't invented a drink yet that would help you over the road I was headed for, but I didn't know that, then.

As Cronin walked out, I waved to the bartender and said, "The usual."

I had the usual, and then I left. It was a wet evening and I shivered with the chill, pulling the collar of my coat up around my neck to keep off the dampness. My car was parked half a block away and I jammed my hands in my pockets and strode away down the rain-slick

11

walks. The streets were deserted; anybody with brains was inside with their shoes off comfortably stretched out before a nice warm television set and slugging a beer before putting the kids to bed and then turning in themselves to share bed and blankets with the better half. It was a warm, pleasant thought and I could recall a time when it was almost more than just a thought for me. But that was a long time and a lot of drinks ago.

It was nice of Cronin to think of me, I reflected, fumbling in a damp pocket for my car keys. Like offering a lush a drink. His job wouldn't help get me back to my book—if anything, it would just take me further away. And that book would join two others gathering dust in my desk drawer.

I got in the car and old Bessie coughed to a waterlogged life. I took the usual route home, to the empty apartment with its usual litter, and tried not to look at the typewriter. As usual, it sat there waiting for me, and as usual, I avoided it, tossing my shirt over it as I undressed for bed.

I smoked the usual last cigarette before I made my usual gesture of switching off the light. Then came the usual darkness, the usual doze, and finally, the usual dream.

That's what came of not drinking enough. When I don't drink enough, I dream. When anybody else dreams they dream of flying or of being the boss while the boss has their job or maybe of making love to their girl friend or the new stenographer who started last week. Or maybe they dream of being caught on the street without their pants on. I don't dream dreams like that. Not any more. My own made-to-order dream came, the usual dream, the one I'd had ever since I got back from the Coast, whenever I went to sleep without enough in me to knock me cold.

As usual, I knew it was only a dream, but that didn't help me. I kept getting hotter and hotter, and I could feel the warmth on my face as I bent down to look at that *other* face, the usual face that was—suddenly, surprisingly, shockingly—*un*usual.

Then I saw it, saw the burned mask with the two blind bubbles oozing up, and I screamed, and my fingernails ripped the sheets to shreds.

I woke up and reached for a cigarette, but I didn't light it. I lay there trembling for a long time, wanting to smoke but not daring to. Because where there's smoke, there's fire.

And I was deathly afraid of fire.

2

I DROVE DOWN to the *Globe* building around ten
the next morning. Even at that hour of the
morning it's playing a deadly game of tag to
navigate the drive along the lake shore. My gut
tightened up like it used to three years before
and I swore at myself for getting mixed up
with something I didn't want to do, money or
no. I had forgotten that Cronin could play
people like violins; he'd catch you in a weak
moment, say the right thing, and you'd make
beautiful music for him.

All the parking spots in front of the *Globe*
were taken and I drove around to the back and
found a spot by the loading docks. Tony on the
freight elevator practically hemorrhaged with
joy when he saw me and I began to feel a

14

touch of nostalgia. Three years ago, before I had decided to try Literature with a capital "L," I had been one of Cronin's sharpest City Hall reporters. It wasn't a bad racket, Cronin was a good boss, and I had never regretted what I learned. There were even times when I thought of going back, and Tony's delight at seeing me made me think about it again. For exactly one-and-three-quarters seconds . . .

Ed Cronin was in his office, waiting for me. He reached for a notebook the moment I walked in.

"All set," he said. "Here's the list."

He handed me a sheet of names, I read it quickly.

The White Brotherhood
Church of the Golden Atom
New Kingdom Tabernacle
Wisdom Center
House of Truth
Temple of the Living Flame

"You'll find the addresses in the notebook," he told me. "And the names of the principals. We've got dope on some of them, and nothing on others. That's your job—to dig up the rest."

I nodded.

"Let me know if you need any help. I can give you a photographer if you tell me a couple hours in advance. And you'll want a press card, I suppose."

My head stopped nodding and started to

shake. "These operators don't care for the press. Wouldn't it be better if I just drifted in and attended the meetings, first? Then, when I got a line on the pitch, I could go back and arrange an interview—know what I was talking about and what I was looking for."

"Could be."

He made a note on a pad. "I'll set up an ad to announce the series. That ought to give the *Chronicle* and the *Leader* a few headaches."

"It might give them a few ideas, too," I said. "I'd better cover as many meetings as possible before the ad tips our plans."

"Suit yourself. All I want is a good series. But be careful."

"What do you mean?"

"Well, some of these cultists are pretty far out." Cronin glanced down at his note-pad. "You carry a gun?"

"Now wait a minute!" I grinned. "This is a big town. We've got a police force, remember?"

Cronin shrugged. He still wasn't looking at me. "Just an idea," he murmured.

I leaned over the desk. "You're a newspaper man. You don't get ideas. You get facts. Why did you make that crack about a gun?"

"Well—" He shifted uneasily in his chair. "When I sent out a couple of the boys to round up preliminary data, they ran into tough sledding in a few places. The Wisdom Center gang tossed one of them out on his can when he started to ask questions. After talking to Peabody—that's the White Brotherhood outfit—

another guy got a couple of anonymous phone calls, telling him to keep his nose out of it. And the Living Flame bunch wouldn't even let anyone in the place. So—"

"So you've been putting on an act along for my benefit," I interrupted. "Is that it? Handing me a line about a press card and a photographer, knowing I'd refuse. And wanting me to, really, because you already tried to get the story with your staff, and it didn't work. That's why you picked me, isn't it, Cronin? Because an outsider might get in where your people couldn't. And because you're pretty sure the word is out already, and they're waiting for someone to come along. They're stirred up, ripe for trouble. What do you expect for your twelve hundred bucks—do you want me to go out and get killed?"

"Now wait a minute—"

"Well, if you do," I said, "I'm your man. Because I can use the money." I picked up the notebook and headed for the door. "See you in the morgue," I said.

Cronin opened his mouth to say something, but no words came out. I've seen them look that way on the rocks at the zoo, before somebody tossed them a fish.

I turned in the doorway and smiled back at him. "Forget it," I told him. "Can't you take a joke? I was only kidding."

Then I went out, still smiling to myself. Sure, I was only kidding. It was just a rib. People don't get themselves killed over a newspaper article any more, not even by cultists. Not in a big city like this one.

Or do they? Driving away, in the car, I remembered some of the things I'd heard out on the Coast. Rumors, and more than rumors. Some of these screwy outfits were big business to those who ran them—and really big, million-dollar enterprises. There was always a risk involved when anyone interfered.

I stopped smiling. Maybe I should carry a gun, at that. Only I knew I wouldn't, even if this turned out to be dangerous.

Maybe that was the real answer. I wanted it to be dangerous, I wanted to get myself knocked off. I'd taken this assignment because of a death-wish—

Crazy. But perhaps I ought to stop in and see Schwarm one of these days now, tell him about it. He'd know.

I filed that idea for future reference, and dumped all the other ideas on top of it. They've never invented a safe as reliable as the good old human skull. It can keep a lot of secrets snug and secure. Of course, lately, some of those head-shrinkers have adopted safe-cracking tactics, boring into the skull with chisels. Nothing's really inviolate any more. You can't hide anything, they always find out, and the dream keeps coming back over and over again until you see what you've tried to lock away, even from yourself. Until you see that charred face—

"Hey, whyncha look where the hell ya goin'?"

I jerked upright as the kid yelled at me, from

the curb. "Sorry," I said, twisting the wheel.
Had to watch myself. Watch where I was
going.

Where *was* I going?

No sense thinking about *that*, either. Except
in the purely superficial sense.

Right now I was going to eat lunch. Afterwards I'd read the notebook and make plans.

I slid into a parking spot, just south of the
business district, and entered the Dinner Gong.
I slid into a booth, slid some food into me, and
started to read over the material in the notes.

The White Brotherhood was first on the list.

*"Rev. Amos Peabody. Claims divinity. Predicts
end of world. 1970. Check previous claim, end of
world 1960. Approx. 200 followers. Gimmick—
sign over all possessions. Res. in Tabernacle, 149
S. Mason. Meetings ev. Tuesday, Thursday, 8
pm."*

This was Tuesday. No sense going over the
rest of the notebook now. I could check on the
White Brotherhood and attend their meeting
tonight; maybe see Peabody himself afterwards,
and get the first story out.

I looked at my watch. Not yet one o'clock. I
got out of the Dinner Gong and headed the
Ford toward the Court House. From there I
went to the Federal Building, and from the
Federal Building to the Public Library.

By the time I got around to looking at my
watch again, it was almost seven. But I had my
notes, plenty of them. I could almost do the
article without seeing a meeting.

Peabody was a pretty standard operator, apparently. I knew now how many times he'd been married, and how many times arrested on suspicion of practising a con game. I knew his income for last year—or what he'd reported—and where it came from. I knew how he ran his racket, and who he'd stolen his pitch from.

I'd met so many of the breed out on the Coast, and so many of the followers. That was the group which really interested me—the followers, the believers, the wonder-seekers, hungry for miracles.

Escape. Everybody wanted escape nowadays. Some found it in a television tube, others sought it in a hypodermic syringe, and it was still selling in pints and fifths.

Nobody wanted reality any more. Reality had been reduced to a simple but unpalatable recipe:

"Take one pinch of hydrogen atoms—add a dash of cobalt—and stand *way* back."

That was the little household hint they were all trying to run away from. Just as sure as death and taxes—and there was plenty of both around for good measure, today.

So, inevitably, some people sought the cults. Certain familiar types to whom spectator-sports and vicarious satisfaction or distraction was not enough. I knew whom I'd find in the ranks of the White Brotherhood.

There was the fat, frowsy housewife, elevated to the circle of the Chosen Ones. The stammering sweeper from the factory, taking his place in the Exalted Hierarchy and gloating over the Day of Doom that awaits the foreman and the bosses. The bespectacled girl with the stringy hair who becomes the Bride of Glory. The aging man whose repentance for past sins increases with his impotence, putting those sins behind him and buying his way to favor in the Coming Kingdom.

These were the people Amos Peabody commanded and commended to the Holy Spirit— all duly incorporated according to law, everything legally protected in his name; a nice, clean, tax-free little setup and growing bigger every day. Give 'em all a title, make 'em feel important, tell 'em everybody else is going to burn while the True Believers get their pie in the sky. Amos Peabody was getting *his* pie right here and now. And perhaps he wouldn't like a stranger to come around and poke a finger into it.

But I drove down to 149 S. Mason just the same, and got there about half past seven. It was just the kind of a setup I expected to find—a big three-story frame building that had once been a public meeting hall, probably. Now the first floor was a tabernacle, and the second and third given over to offices and living-quarters. Everything looked simple and unpretentious enough—but that was deliberate on Peabody's part. Never scare the suckers away with a flash front, not if you're working the "end of the world" racket and preaching the renunciation of all earthly possessions.

Most of the chumps probably didn't know what I'd learned in just one afternoon's work. They weren't aware that Mr. Peabody owned an eighty-acre estate out in the Heights and lived in a fourteen-room mansion. They knew he had two Cadillacs and an ermine robe, because they'd given him these gifts by subscription; a prophet is supposed to enjoy a few luxuries. But they wouldn't figure on finding all that money in real estate and in bonds—not when Peabody was spreading the glad tidings about the end of the world.

I stared at the front of the building as the lights went on. Half an hour early, but they were getting ready. Little knots of people were eddying on the walk just outside. A few older people, a surprising number of youthful ones— the good clean-cut youngsters in conservative suits and cheery smiles just a few years away from executive trainee programs and YMCA secretary-ships. Outwardly, at least, they were identical in size and shape to young Episcopalians or Methodists or Christian Scientists or Knights of Columbus. Inwardly, the mixture was probably a little different. A little guiltier, perhaps. Oddball personalities that found their sense of belonging in an oddball religious off-shoot . . .

I glanced at my watch. Time for me to get ready. Half an hour to go. All at once I remembered that I hadn't eaten anything since lunch time.

Maybe I could pick up a sandwich in a hurry. I glanced down the block and realized my luck wasn't going to be very good. Once away from the yellow pool of light in front of the scrubbed white of the tabernacle, I was out of the high-rent district. Faded buildings with peeling paint, dirty, fly-specked plate-glass windows, second-hand furniture stores, a magazine store with a sign advertising old books and magazines in both English and Spanish, a run-down movie theater shilling for that great hit, "Los Níños Encantados." A candy store, still open, with a couple of kids in black leather jackets and hair to match, lounging out in front and digging the squares in front of the tabernacle.

A wind came up and old newspapers went skittering down the dusty streets; half a block away there was the sudden clatter of a garbage can and the surprised yowl of a cat. I could smell rain in the air and glanced at the sky to note the full-rigged clouds sailing slowly past the moon. Fine night, I thought. For a lot of things. All of them bad . . .

The one beanery on the block was closed and I decided to try a bar. In a neighborhood like this, tavern neon always seems to burn brighter by way of contrast.

I walked across the street and down the block to the bar. *Joe's Place*. Why is it that nine out of ten taverns are identified by the first name of the proprietor? What is there about our life and times that makes us feel we must be on a first-name basis with the bartender?

Why is a raven like a writing-desk?

Lewis Carroll knew a lot about Wonderland, and I'll bet he never entered a tavern in his life. But I wasn't Lewis Carroll. I was Phil Dempster, and I didn't live in Wonderland.

I went into the tavern.

It was a Mom-and-Pop setup, with Joe behind the bar, reading the sports page. When I asked about a sandwich he said sure, and called Mom. She was in the back room, and after she took the order she returned there to slice the liver-sausage.

I had a bottle of beer while I waited. I found out I was thirsty, too, so I had another. Then the sandwich arrived, and something which Mom called coffee. The old girl had quite an imagination.

Two gulps and I put the cup down. I called for a shot, instead. At least I could believe the labels on the bottles.

I took another look at my notes. Everything seemed to be in order. Maybe I could leave the notebook here when I went over to the White Brotherhood. I wanted to make sure the stuff was safe.

Not that I really expected to run into trouble. Still, you never could tell. No sense taking chances. Taking chances on getting tossed out, or roughed up, or—

What was the matter with me? Didn't I want to go? Didn't I want to earn that money? After all, as Cronin said, this would be a public service. Exposing a charlatan, saving people from being deceived by a fast operator who wouldn't hesitate for a moment to cut your throat and—

All right. So I *didn't* want to go. I knew that, now. I'd lost my nerve. That's why I couldn't write any more, that's why I was afraid of my own shadow.

No, not my shadow. I was afraid of something else, and Cronin knew it. I knew it, too. I was afraid, and so I was drinking.

I was drinking now. Five minutes to eight, and I'd just ordered another shot. Two shots and two beers on an almost empty stomach. That ought to give me the courage to go through with it.

But I kept hoping I wouldn't have to. That something would save me, at the last minute. *Save me, save me,* the voice kept saying it over and over again in my head. I knew the voice and wanted to forget it. Another drink would help. Only there wasn't time.

I started to get up, got ready to pay up and ask Joe if he'd please hang onto my stuff for me for an hour or so.

Then the door opened.

The door opened, and this girl walked in.

She didn't belong in a Mom-and-Pop tavern. She didn't belong in this neighborhood, or even in this world. I knew where she belonged. She belonged in my dreams—the ones I used to have, a long, long time ago.

Her hair was copper, the color of a newly-minted penny; the kind you put in your pocket for good luck. And she was almost, but not quite, pocket-size. Rather short, but after a single glance you didn't notice it, because she was perfectly proportioned. Meaning that the lines of her black wool dress were moulded to her body, that the white curve of her throat drew the eye irresistibly down to delight the—

I blinked and shook my head. This wasn't *like* me. I hadn't even thought about women since I came back from the Coast. Up until now, if anyone had asked, I'd have told them I didn't intend to think about them again.

But here I was, and here *she* was. Why? How had she strayed into this cheap joint, what was she doing here?

It was none of my business, but I watched her as she walked over to the bar and ordered a drink. Bourbon, on the rocks. The bartender didn't know her, that was obvious. He poured, and I stared. Stared until she became conscious of my scrutiny, and turned to face me.

I caught a glimpse of green eyes. Then she glanced away. Sure, why not? This was real life. In real life no dream-girl ever walks up to you and says, "You must be Phil Dempster. I've always wanted to meet you."

I caught her staring at me again, and turned away. Time to talk to the bartender. He came down the line and I leaned over.

Then I felt the hand on my shoulder. I looked around and she was standing there. Standing there and smiling, and saying, "Pardon me. But aren't you Philip Dempster? You know, I've always wanted to meet you."

3

LET'S NOT FORGET our fuse. It was burning now, but I didn't know it, didn't realize how quickly a spark can travel. Even if I'd known, the chances are I wouldn't have done anything about it.

If you've ever seen a fuse burn, perhaps you can understand why. You get so that you forget about the danger and just look at the spark— the little red spark, eating its way along, moving so prettily, so swiftly, so magically. You watch the spark, and it's like something alive. Unconsciously, you *identify* yourself with it, find yourself hoping it will keep on living instead of going out. And the spark moves on, and on, faster and faster, until the explosion.

At the time, though, I was unaware. All I

knew was that a dream was happening. One of the good dreams, one of the best.

And the dream said, "I thought I recognized you, but I wasn't sure. You look just like your picture on the dust-jacket."

Then I understood, and it wasn't a dream any more. "So you read the book," I said.

"Certainly. We bought three copies for the library."

"Are you a librarian?"

"Not any more. I used to be. I'm working as a private secretary now." She gave me a look from under her lowered lashes. "But this isn't very polite, is it—just coming up to you this way without even introducing myself."

"Let's be honest," I said. "I love it. Doesn't happen very often—people don't remember the names of writers. You were a librarian, you ought to know that. Somebody will go on and on about a book they've read. Ask them who wrote it and they can't tell you."

"That's right, Mr. Dempster."

"What are you drinking, Miss—?"

"Bourbon."

"I see. And the name?"

"Diana Rideaux." She spelled it for me.

"French, eh?"

"My father was. Creole, rather—I was born in New Orleans."

"Wonderful city. I'm going back there some day," I told her. "Always wanted to do a definitive study of the old voodoo cults. Know anything about that?"

"No. I've lived up here most of my life."

Glancing over to the bar, I gave Joe a nod. "Two bourbons," I said. "On the rocks."

Joe brought the drinks. We made small talk. I found out that she had come down here to visit an aunt, but the aunt was out. And she'd forgotten to bring a coat, and it was chilly on the corner waiting for the bus, so she stopped in for a quick drink to warm her up. She wasn't in the habit of going into strange taverns or any taverns, alone, and she hoped I didn't have the wrong impression.

I assured her that I did not, that I had a very good impression. Which was quite true. The more I saw, the more I liked. And then she got to talking about the novel, and the more I heard, the more I liked.

Then I glanced at my watch, and it was quarter after eight. She noticed how I checked the time and said, "Am I keeping you from an engagement?"

"No, not at all. There's no place I'd rather be than right here." Which was also true. I was beginning to get a glow. Some of it came from the liquor. Some of it came from her presence; the nearness of that copper cloud, all warm and soft and scented.

It was very pleasant to sit there, drink in hand, and listen to a pretty girl talk about me. That may sound very fatuous, but I've got a hunch every man feels that way, really. Even though most of them would be ashamed to admit it.

I really should break it off, I kept telling myself. Maybe make another date for another time. I had to get over to that meeting.

But then again, suppose I missed a few minutes? Probably didn't start on time, anyway. Eight-thirty would be soon enough. We could have another drink, first.

So we did, and Miss Rideaux suggested we move into a booth, because now some of the regular customers had come in. We moved to the booth and went on talking.

By the time I checked my watch again it was quarter to nine. And we'd just ordered another drink.

There really wasn't any hurry, come to think of it. The White Brotherhood would be holding another jam-session on Thursday night. That would be soon enough; I could cover it then. Why leave now, just when everything was going so smoothly, floating along on a sea of bourbon and perfume?

I felt better than I had in months, better than I thought I'd ever feel again. This was perfect. There are some girls you like to talk to, and some girls you like to drink with; but the trouble is, one kind resents the other. Besides, it's very expensive to take two girls out at the same time, even if they *are* willing. Which they aren't.

So I was lucky, getting the combination rolled into one. A librarian who liked libations. And who stimulated the libido. Yes, indeed— almost too good to be true. That's what I'd told Margery once. "You're too good to be true. Promise that you'll be true."

"What's wrong?" she said. I realized that Miss Rideaux was staring at me. "Did I say something?"

"No. Why?" I asked.

"You're frowning."

"Sorry. I just remembered something—"

"I'll bet you did have a date tonight after all."

"Not a date," I said. "An assignment."

"Assignment? What do you mean?"

So I told her about the White Brotherhood. Somewhere along the line we had another drink, and then another. What was it—number seven or number eight? I was losing count now, but it didn't matter. Nothing mattered except that I was talking to her and she was listening and leaning forward so that I could smell her perfume and smell her hair and stare into those green eyes, those smoky emeralds, no, more like jade, copper and jade—

But I didn't tell her about that, of course. I was being very brilliant and very analytical about cults. Everything is very brilliant and very analytical after the eighth drink, or was this the tenth coming up now? Anyway, I told her all about the White Brotherhood, and she was quite interested. I explained to her why people joined such organizations, what the attraction was. I told her about some of the coast outfits in the past—the *I Am* movement, and *Mankind United;* Arthur Bell and Riker,

Kullgren, and the Man from Lemuria down in Ojai. Bell's take was better than two and a half million dollars in ten years. And the *I Am* deal grossed even more.

"Started out back in the '30s," I said. "Man name of Guy Ballard and his wife were leaders. He was a former paper-hanger. Wrote this book, *Unveiled Mysteries*, under the pseudonym of Godfrey Ray King. Ever read it?"

She shook her head. *That* was something to see. It made me want to reach out and touch her hair. Instead, I kept on talking.

"Ballard just happened to be climbing Mount Shasta one fine day when he ran into Saint Germain, the Ascended Master. Saint Germain give Ballard a drink of something called electronic essence and a tablet of the same stuff— remember, this was before the day of vitamin pills. Must have been a pretty powerful mixture, because white flames shot out fifty feet in the air on all sides of him, and he was levitated through space. Saint Germain took him on a conducted tour of Egypt, South America, India and Yellowstone National Park—showed him the location of ancient cities filled with hoards of buried treasure. Told him that there were other Ascended Masters who lived eternally in the secret places of the earth and directed its destiny. Now the time had come to reveal the truth to all, and Ballard had been selected to bring the message to the world." I paused, sipped my drink, offered her a cigarette.

"No thanks. Go on—this is interesting."

"The best is yet to come," I told her. "Ballard went home and started to write his book. Saint Germain dictated some of it to him, and he kept on through the years—but I don't think he ever got a share of the royalties. Ballard handled the money, and did pretty well.

"He set up a temple, of course, and he sold signet rings, and steel engravings of Cosmic Beings. He had a cold cream, too, and charts and books and even phonograph records of the 'music of the spheres'. There was a monthly magazine and printed lectures and study courses.

"He had classes going in his Sanctuary from seven in the morning until midnight. The pupils learned chants, and the secret of color vibrations. They bought everything, including a 'Flame in Action' machine which sold for a couple of hundred dollars."

"Fantasy," said Miss Rideaux.

"Reality," I told her. "This actually happened—it's all down in the records. You see, the pupils were learning the words and colors and prayers which would remove the layer of Evil from the earth. Saint Germain and the other Ascended Masters helped out with the Purple Ray. Once this layer was removed, everybody could attain heart's desire. You could get a 'precipitation' of anything you wanted. All you did was concentrate on the object until it appeared. If you wanted a new washing machine, 'precipitation' would give it to you.

"And there were other benefits. Didn't Ballard

predict the destruction of Southern California in 1936, and them save it by pleading with Saint Germain at the last minute? Didn't he sink three submarines Hitler had sent to blow up the Panama Canal? Didn't he offer them all immortality and riches? They got their money's worth, all right."

"How did Ballard make out?" the girl asked.

"Not too badly. You see, the cult spread to other cities. At one time he had over three hundred thousand followers. If Ballard hadn't died, and if his wife hadn't been convicted of using the mails to defraud, it might have gone on to greater heights. Anyhow, when the Feds stepped in and took an audit many years ago, they estimated Ballard's take at way over three million dollars."

"Three million—!"

"Not bad for electronic essence," I said. "How about another drink?"

She nodded. The drinks didn't seem to bother her at all, but they were getting to me. When I take on a little too much alcohol my speech centers aren't affected, but my vision goes haywire.

Right now she was nothing but a copper blur. Not bright and shiny, but dim and wavering. I told myself that maybe I needed glasses. I told myself that maybe I didn't need what was *in* glasses. Not very funny. I laughed anyway.

"Mr. Dempster—is something the matter?"

"No, nothing. Just too much electronic essence, I guess. Can I drive you home?"

She stared at me and I tried to stare back. I could tell she was shaking her head.

"No. I don't think so. But if you've got a car outside, *I'll* drive *you* home."

"Sorry. I shouldn't have taken that last one. I've been drinking too much lately. Got to cut it out." I stood up.

"Think you can make it all right?" Her hand, on my arm.

"Of course I can." And I could. I walked out of there under my own power. The place was crowded now, and nobody paid any attention to us. She went first, and I followed the copper blur.

In the car I could close my eyes. I gave her my address and she drove. I guess I fell asleep for a little while, because when I came to we were parked in front of the apartment. She was opening the car door.

"Going to leave it out all night?" she asked.

"Sure. I've got a permit."

"Then I'll be on my way." She smiled, or I thought she did. "And thank you for a very entertaining evening."

Entertaining, hell. What's this modern generation coming to, I asked myself. Used to be that the woman had a few too many and the man took her home—or somewhere. And now the whole deal was reversed. *She* took *me* home. Fine thing. Phil Dempster meets his dream girl and ends up with a jag on, too woozy to even think of asking her to come upstairs—

"Hey," I said. "Where are you going?"

"Home, naturally. I live over on Fairhope. Don't worry, there's a bus stop right at the corner."

"I'm sorry," I sighed. "I'm a mess."

"Don't be sorry. I enjoyed it."

"Well, I didn't. Next time I promise—" I leaned forward. "Can I phone you?"

"Of course. I'm in the book."

"Stay home tomorrow night. I'll call."

"That'll be fine. Goodnight." She hesitated a moment. "Are you sure you can make it upstairs?"

"Sure. I'm all right, I—"

But she was gone. I heard her heels clattering away, and I leaned out the window to look, only everything was blurred. Everything was blurred, and I'd been lying. I wasn't all right. I was all wrong, *this* was wrong, this drinking and drinking and drinking every night because of a dream that wasn't real. When a reality came along I wasn't ready for it; I kept on drinking and let her go.

Why hadn't we just talked? Why hadn't I found out a few things about her, instead of doing all that ranting over a bunch of crazy cults? As it was, she must think I was just a stewbum—typical drunken writer. The kind of guy she was glad to get rid of.

As it was, she hadn't told me a thing. She was a private secretary, yes, but where? Lived

on Fairhope, she said, but what address?
Probably roomed with someone, and I'd never
know now.

Still, she'd given me her phone number,
hadn't she? No—she hadn't. Just said I could
call her tomorrow night. In the book, she told
me. And that was probably a stall, to get away
from here fast.

Why didn't I think to ask the number, write
it down in the notebook? The notebook—

I felt in my pockets. Nothing there. I groped
around on the seat beside me, scrabbled at the
floor under my feet. Then I remembered.

I left the notebook back in the tavern, in the
booth.

That was it. I *must* have. And I had to get it.
What if somebody from the White Brotherhood
drifted into Joe's Place after the meeting and
found my notes?

I had to get it. She was gone now, the bus
had thundered past five minutes ago. Nobody
to drive me. Late. I didn't see a taxi. Maybe I
could go upstairs and call one—

No. That might take a half-hour or more, this
time of night. The sooner I got my hands on
the notebook the better. I could drive the car
myself. I was all right.

*For a while the fuse seems to burn slowly, and
then at the last the spark just races along—*

I slid over in the seat, groped for the keys in
the ignition. The car began to purr and throb,
purr and throb, crawl forward and then streak
through the night like a cat pouncing on its

prey. A copper cat, with green eyes. The cat-goddess of Bubastis. There was a cult idea—revive the ancient Egyptian pantheon. Didn't some associate of Aleister Crowley try that? Crowley was a devil-worshipper. The Great Beast 666, he called himself. And people believed. Everybody believed nowadays, everybody heard voices, everybody saw visions.

Even I saw them when I dreamed, and there was no sense shutting my eyes. Can't drive now with your eyes shut—

I came to, somewhere on Fuller Avenue. A voice was whispering to me, "You can't make it, Phil. You can't make it. Why don't you stop, stop, stop?"

It was my own voice, and I didn't want to listen. I didn't want to stop. I *had* to make it. Even though I couldn't see what I was doing, where I was going.

Something was wrong with me, something was terribly wrong. If Schwarm were here, he'd know. He'd tell me what to do. He'd tell me to go home, and I'd go. Or he'd tell me to park, get out and walk the rest of the way before I ran into someone.

That was it. I could get out and walk. Only a few blocks more to go. Safer to walk. Then I wouldn't kill anybody, or take a chance on killing myself.

It had started to drizzle and I was dimly aware of the dampness on my face. I didn't bother buttoning my coat or trying to keep the chill off. In one sense I hoped the rain would

sober me up. But that was a faraway thought
and in another larger sense, I really didn't care
whether I sobered up. Then, or ever. The walks
were slippery and once I almost fell and
thought vaguely I should watch it or I'd hurt
myself. Or bump into somebody and hurt
them . . .

I didn't want to hurt anyone, I didn't want to
kill anyone. I didn't want to die. I didn't want
to *see* anyone die. That was it. That was the
most important thing. Not to *see* anyone die.

So I walked, with my eyes closed. And my
mind closed. I just walked, and then I guess I
must have climbed. I know, there at the last,
that I ran.

I ran through a blackout, because everything
was getting too clear all of a sudden—too clear,
and too bright. I could see too well.

There was a time when I stood in front of a
door and rattled the knob. Was it Joe's tavern,
was it closed?

There was a time when I went somewhere
else and walked with my eyes shut, praying for
another moment of peace before I opened them
and realized what my awakened senses were
trying to tell me—before I had to see what I
could smell now, and hear.

The fuse sputters loudly at the end—

But this wasn't a sputtering. This was a low
murmur that became a roar. A roaring in my
ears, and a choking in my lungs. It was behind
me now, I was moving away, I was running
away to the corner.

Something red stood on the corner. I opened my eyes just long enough to see it. Something red, shining in the reflection of the light that came from behind me.

I went over to it, hung onto it. My hand went out and up, finding pain and then warmth. My hand moved then, and I heard a sound.

Then the sound was drowned out in the roaring, and the roaring was drowned out in the wailing. I slumped there, wanting to pass out but not quite making it. Maybe a minute passed, maybe five, maybe ten.

And all at once somebody was shaking me, I was awake, I was sober. But how can a man be awake and sober in a nightmare?

I didn't know.

All I know is that's how they found me, standing there next to the fire-alarm on the corner, while the tabernacle of the White Brotherhood went up in flames behind me.

4

IT WAS just beginning to get light outside. I could see the first streaks of dawn through the high window in the little office.

Captain Dalton pushed a mug of coffee my way. I picked it up and took a mouthful. It had a bitter taste, like ashes. Everything tasted of ashes, smelled of smoke to me.

"All right, Mr. Dempster," he said. "We're ready for that statement."

"But I told you everything. And I told Detective Henderson on the way down here—"

"This is for the record. Official." The short, grey-haired head of the Arson Squad stabbed the stem of his pipe toward the stenographer who sat beside me, pad in hand.

I wondered what on earth could induce a

man to take such a job—sit there ready for
dictation at five in the morning. I wondered
why the head of the Arson Squad was allowed
to smoke a pipe. I wondered about a lot of
things.

"Try to remember every detail, now. This is
serious."

I nodded. It was serious, all right. Serious as
hell. The red hell of a holocaust, walls coming
down in a shower of sparks—three alarms at
the last, with the streets roped off all around.
They found Peabody's body in a room upstairs,
and three others; members of the White Brotherhood who were sleeping there overnight. The
whole building had burned up. Burned to
the ground. How can something burn up to the
ground? O, it was serious, I knew that. And I
knew that they hadn't bothered to bring me
down here just for the ride. I'd already talked to
a detective and to the Fire Marshal, too. If the
Arson Squad was in on it, that meant they
suspected—

"Where should I begin?" I asked.

"Start with this evening. I want a full
statement. The works."

I gave him the works. Who I was, what I was
doing. I told him about Ed Cronin and my
assignment. I told him about going into Joe's
tavern. I told him about meeting Diana Rideaux,
and what had happened. About her driving me
home, and me going back for the notebook.

That is, I told him about my physical actions
of the evening. I didn't mention how much I

had to drink, or what the drinks had done to me. I didn't tell him how I'd walked around with my eyes shut, or where I had walked. Partly because there were long stretches I couldn't remember, and partly because there were other stretches I didn't want to remember. Certainly I wouldn't talk about those things.

It was enough to say I'd gone back to the tavern, found it locked, then noticed the flames, smelled the smoke, and turned in the alarm.

Or *was* it enough?

When I'd finished talking, Captain Dalton looked at me. "That's it?" he asked.

"That's it."

He glanced down at a sheet of paper. "Couple of other points you might be able to help us on," he said. "According to what Henderson put down here, you didn't drive all the way to the tavern. Instead, you parked over on Fuller, in the 300 block. Why?"

"I told you. I'd had a few drinks too many, thought the air might do me good."

He nodded. "So you went straight over to the tavern and found it closed."

My turn to nod.

"What did you figure on doing then? Going straight home and calling the tavern in the morning?"

I nodded again.

"I see." Captain Dalton stabbed at the notes with his pipe. "You're sure that's all you had in mind?"

"Of course. What else was there to do?"

"That's what I'm asking you." Dalton stood up. He was a short man, but at the moment he looked quite tall as he stood peering down at me. "Because if you were going right home, you'd walk back to the car, wouldn't you? And the car was in the *other* direction from the White Brotherhood tabernacle. Yet you didn't go back—you went forward. You had to go forward, because we found you on the far corner after the alarm was turned in."

"I saw the flames," I said. "I smelled smoke."

He kept staring at me. "What time was this?"

"Never thought to look. I'd been drinking, you know how it is."

"I don't know how it is. I want to find out." He turned away. "Would you say you put in the alarm immediately?"

"Of course. Wasn't that the thing to do?"

He didn't answer me directly. He talked to the wall, now. "If you turned it in at once, then somebody's cockeyed."

"What do you mean?"

"The alarm went in at exactly one-fifteen. That's on record. You say you went straight from the tavern to the alarm box, because you smelled smoke and saw flames. Is that correct?"

"Yes."

"How long would you estimate it would take to walk from the tavern door to the alarm?"

"Three minutes. Maybe less."

He was staring at me again. "Three minutes, maybe less." Now the pipe-stem was stabbing straight at my eyes. "So according to your story, you must have tried that tavern door at around ten after one. At eleven after, or twelve after, you looked down the block and saw flames. From the front window upstairs, you said."

"That's right."

Captain Dalton went over to the side door and opened it. He called into the next room. "Bring Shelby in for a minute, will you?"

A detective entered, followed by a bespectacled man wearing a cab-driver's cap and a leather jacket.

"You're Mr. Shelby?" asked the Captain.

"Yeah, I'm Vick Shelby."

"My name's Dalton. Arson Squad. I read your statement."

The cab-driver shifted his weight from his right leg to his left. "What's the matter with it? I tole you evvything I know. Look, I gotta get outta here, I gotta check in—"

"There's nothing wrong. You'll be released in just a moment. But first, I wanted you to go over it again, so I could hear for myself. You say you were coming down Mason at ten after one?"

"That's right. I turned off Claybourne at ezacally ten after. Reason I remember is this time-load come over the radio for me. One-thirty out at the airport. I called in and give the operator the word, and rules are you gotta say what time it is you get the call. So I says one-ten, see? Then I drove south on Mason, like I said."

"Let me see, now. Claybourne is about a mile north of the White Brotherhood tabernacle, isn't it?"

"Fourteen blocks, countin' the alley off the YMCA."

"And this would bring you abreast of the tabernacle at about one-twelve or one-thirteen?"

"Uh-huh."

"Did you see any flames when you passed the building?"

"No."

"Smell any smoke?"

"No." Vick Shelby shifted from his left foot to his right again. "Diden' I tell you before, if I'd seen anything I would of stopped and put in an alarm? Whaddya gettin' at—tryin' to make me say *I* set the place on fire?"

"Of course not." Captain Dalton was being very kind and very patient; he didn't point his pipe at Vick once. "Just one thing more. As you drove along, did you happen to notice anybody walking, or running, along the left-hand side of the street in the block before the tabernacle?"

"Not a soul," said the cab-driver. "Nobody was around."

"You didn't see a man in front of the alarm box on the corner, either?"

"I didn't see no one."

Dalton was pointing at me again. "You're sure you didn't see *this* man?"

"Never seen him before in my life."

"All right, Mr. Shelby. You can go now, and thanks very much. If we need you, we'll get in touch."

"Okay."

And out he went. Just opened the door and walked out, free as the air. While I sat there, and the pipe-stem pointed.

"You didn't see the cab go by, did you?"

"Of course not. I would have mentioned it if I had. I told you everything I know."

"Did you?" Dalton sat down again. He was beginning to sweat a little, I noticed, but I didn't care. Because I was wringing wet, myself.

"Did you?" Dalton repeated. "You say you were at the tavern at one-ten or a moment later. That you walked down Mason Street and crossed over immediately, seeing flames at one-twelve or one-thirteen. But the cab-driver didn't see any flames at that time. And he didn't see you, either."

"I can't help that," I said. "Maybe I was in the shadows. Maybe there was some kind of explosion and the flames broke out suddenly, in a moment or so. I wouldn't have waited a second to call after I saw them."

"Wouldn't you, Mr. Dempster?"

"Say, what is this? Do you think *I* started the fire?" My voice sounded just like the cab-driver's.

"I don't think anything." He sighed. "I

haven't even said I thought anyone *started* the fire. It could have been spontaneous combustion, for all we know. But it's our business to find out. Our business, because the place wasn't covered by any insurance. If the National Board of Fire Underwriters was in on this deal, you'd really be getting some questions along about now."

"Look," I said. "I told you what I know about it. And I told you I was under the weather. A man doesn't always remember details. Maybe I got there earlier and walked around a while. But I did see flames, I did turn in the alarm. Since when is it a crime to turn in a fire-alarm at a fire?" I stood up. "Since when is it a crime to park your car down the street and take a little walk? I didn't set fire to that place. Why should I? I'd never even been there in my life. Think it over, it doesn't make sense!"

"Nothing makes sense," Dalton told me. "You start out for a meeting, but you don't go. You meet a strange girl and hang one on with her. Know her name but not where she lives. She drives you home, but you come back because you forgot your notebook. Only you don't come back all the way. You park your car down the street and walk. You claim all this happened just before the fire broke out. But why couldn't it have been earlier? Suppose you came back at twelve-thirty instead of ten after one and you—"

"Why?" I was almost shouting at him. "You

tell me for a change. What's the reason, what's the motive? Every crime's got to have a motive."

Dalton tapped his pipe on the desk and shook his head. "That's the odd part of it," he murmured. His voice was soft, reflective. "Arson, yes. We get motives galore. Insurance is the biggest one, of course. Then there's revenge—discharged employee burning down the plant because he's mad at the boss. There's jealousy, too, and sometimes fire is a cover-up for murder. Lots of motives like that. Not all of them seem completely sane or rational reasons, but we can understand them. It's the other kind we're afraid of. The cases where there is no motive, no sense. The torch doesn't have a reason for setting fires—at least, not one he can understand. Voices tell him to do it, or he likes to see things burn, or he wants to watch the firemen come and maybe even run into the flames himself and be a hero. Many times a firebug doesn't even seem to realize what he's done—it's as though the whole experience was blotted out of his consciousness."

"Sounds crazy to me," I said.

"It is crazy." Dalton began to load his pipe. "There's a name for it too. They call it pyromania."

"You can't lean on me," I whispered, whispering because I was frightened. "You said yourself you don't even know if the fire *was* started by somebody. You haven't got a crime, let alone a criminal. If you want to book me, I want a chance to call a lawyer. But I've told you the truth. You can check with Ed Cronin, check with that girl—"

The door opened and the detective who'd brought the cab-driver stuck his head in.

"Girl's here," he said.

Dalton frowned at him, then rose. "Right with you," he said. And then, to me, "You stay here until I get back. Keep an eye on him, Scotty."

The stenographer nodded.

I sat there and watched the dawn come up. The beautiful, beautiful dawn. Coming up like fire—

Then I closed my eyes. *Pyromania. Sometimes you don't even realize what you've done. How long had I walked around and where had I gone? Burning. That charred mask—*

What was going on out there? What was he asking Diana Rideaux, what was she telling him?

I don't know if he was gone five minutes or five hours. The sun was shining in my eyes when he came back in. The detective was with him.

"All right, Dempster," he said. "You can run along home now. But stick around town in case we want to call you later."

I stood up, nodded. "Where's Miss Rideaux?" I asked.

"She just left. But it's all right. Her story checks you out. According to her, she didn't say

51

goodnight to you until one o'clock. Lucky for you she was around."

I had trouble standing. My feet were asleep. Captain Dalton came over to me. "All right?" he asked.

"Sure. Fine."

"Sorry I went after you that way. But you've got to be careful in this line of work. I've seen some mighty funny cases. Nothing screwier than a firebug."

"I understand." I moved away. The detective put his hand on my arm.

"Want to take the back way out?" he asked. "Reporters up front."

I nodded gratefully.

"I'll have one of the squads drive you home," he said. "This must have been rough on you." He fished in his pocket, pulled out a pack of cigarettes. "Here—have one?"

"No, thanks," I answered. "I've given up smoking."

5

I WANTED TO SLEEP, now, but there was too
much to do. The first job was to take a cab
over to Joe's tavern. It was open, and Joe was
there.

So was my notebook.

"Noticed it when I come to clear away the
glasses after you left," he said. "Too late to call
you. Figured you'd be back."

"Thanks," I said.

"Detective was in here asking after it. He
looked at it, I guess, but he didn't take it
along. Got something to do with the fire?"

"Didn't you read it?"

Joe indicated the crowded bar. "Who's got
time to read, business like this? Besides—it
ain't my proppity."

I was willing to accept his first reason. The bar seemed to be doing a rushing morning business. So was the street, outside. Plenty of traffic, plenty of spectators, plenty of morbid curiosity-seekers come to gape at the still smoking ruins. People are always interested in fires. Why?

"No kidding," Joe said. "You have somethin' to do with the fire?"

"Sure," I told him. "I set it."

"Ah—"

"Thanks for the notebook. Look, hadn't you better be getting back to the customers?"

"Ma'll handle 'em." He leaned over the bar. "Didja see it burn, huh?"

"No. I was home."

"Boy, that was really somethin'! Flames musta been thirty feet in the air. They had five engines here—we was roped off, they wouldn't let us get any closer. Ma and me, we watched outta the window upstairs, though. You could feel the heat way over here."

I edged away from the bar, seeking escape.

"You heard about Peabody, huh? Him and three other guys got it. Jeez, that must be a awful way to die—"

This wasn't what I wanted to hear. I had to make him stop. "Did you know Peabody?" I asked.

"Him? Nah. He never come in here. Didn't even take a glass of beer. None of that gang ever showed around. Bunch a fanatics, you ask me. Give all their money to the Brotherhood. Big racket. How can people get so crazy?"

I shook my head. I didn't know how people could get so crazy. Yesterday I thought I did, but today I wasn't sure any more. Wasn't sure what being crazy meant. Did it mean you wanted to start fires, did it mean you wanted to watch fires, did it mean you were afraid of fire? If so, then everyone was crazy.

"Sorry," I said. "I've got to go. My car's parked down the street."

He opened his mouth, but I opened the door. And once again, I started walking in the wrong direction.

I *had* to see it before I went away.

The actual intersection was still roped off, and the fire department was very much in evidence; their vehicles and men were scattered all over the place.

The curbs were lined with parked cars for blocks around, and a sizeable crowd pressed against the ropes. Cops walked back and forth, ordering the spectators to stand clear, move along. But they grinned as they spoke, and the crowd grinned back.

There was an air of holiday gaiety here. I didn't sense any carefree happiness, but I could feel the excitement and the exhilaration. I shouldered my way up to the rope, and all around me people were smiling and staring.

I stared, too, but I didn't smile. The gutted core of the tabernacle still stood, although the two walls on the farther side had toppled almost from the foundation. The roof was gone, of course, but the front remained upright— empty windows like blind eyes, the open door like a burned mouth from which poured a stench of ashy decay. Shreds of burned lath and plaster hung in front of the empty window sockets like the greasy hair of a juvenile delinquent. Half the street was cluttered with debris left there when the roof had fallen in and chairs and papers and half-burned hymnals had puffed out of the burning building like dust blown out of a doorway. Something else in the street caught my eye and I almost lost my lunch. It had been an old building and harbored more than its share of the minor animal life that manages to live in symbiosis with urban humanity. Small spiders and bugs had probably gone up like bits of paper on a blast furnace. Then a small army of squealing, burning rats had made a run for it and some had gotten as far as the street outside. I started to shake. Human beings would burn just as easily. And they'd look the same way . . .

Firemen poked around in the ruins, and hose-men near the corner trained a spitting serpent on the cellarway.

This was it, this was the spot where the flames had lived and men had died.

And the crowd liked it. I could see it in their faces. Could see what they felt openly, knew what they felt secretly. The crowd liked it. The Great Beast. The Great Beast who lives on a diet of violence, has lived on it through the centuries.

These were the faces that lighted up in the red reflection of a burning Rome. These were the faces that kindled with glee as the torch was applied to the Christian martyrs—as the faggots fired about the feet of Torquemada's victims. In their eyes I could read the rope, see the stake, learn the love of lynching and the burning desire to burn. This was the Mob, and to the Mob all suffering was a spectacle, all destruction a delight.

Sure, they were talking about how terrible it was. They always talk that way, like old women going on at a funeral. But the old women go to funerals every day, and the Mob goes to scenes of violence and disaster. Goes and gloats. Goes and feasts upon the filth. *Supp'd full with horrors*, isn't that the way Shakespeare puts it?

Give us this day our daily dread. Blasphemy? Perhaps, but there was blasphemy all around me. I could feel the thoughts, the dark desires.

"Glad it wasn't me ... I wish I could have seen it, though ... wonder what it's like to start a fire, burn a place down ... too bad the whole neighborhood didn't go up, then there'd really be something to watch ..."

It had happened at all times, all over the world. They burned the Library at Alexandria, and they burned Rome, and Paris, and London, and Atlanta. Chicago and San Francisco had gone up in flames, too. And always, the Mob came. The Mob came to savor smoke as incense, to view the burnt offering and offer adoration to what dark gods of death? They'd stand there and watch the flames flickering orange and pink and blue and white and feel the warmth on their faces and oooh and aaah when the ceiling fell in or a wall collapsed. They'd quietly root for the flames and silently boo the firemen and stare without pity or sympathy when a volunteer staggered to the sidelines to cough the smoke out of his lungs. It didn't matter whether it was the impersonal facade of the State National Bank being destroyed by the licking flames or Uncle Harry's lingerie shop. There was no pity for the owners, no pity for the victims. Only a sea of too-bright, blazing eyes, the Mob worshipping its oldest god.

I knew. I *knew*. Underneath the gay assertions—"I always look out of the window when I hear the fire-engines go by" and "I don't know what gets into Tom, the minute he hears the siren, off he goes in his car" and "There's just, oh, something about a fire that gets me"—underneath the commonplace, everyday expressions of opinion there was a need. A flaming need for a flaming deed. We're all fire-worshippers at heart. And we rejoice when we see a sacrifice.

Fine thoughts for early morning, after a sleepless night. I shivered and turned away to seek a route to the car.

It was still standing there. I had the keys in my pocket, and the cops hadn't towed it away.

I drove to the apartment, picking up some rolls and a dozen eggs on the way. I made breakfast, shaved, washed.

Then I called Cronin.

"Dempster. You heard about last night?"

"*Heard about it? My God, we're swamped down here!* And where were you, why didn't you phone in the story when it happened?"

"You know why. You must have checked with Dalton by this time."

"Yeah. I know. Fine thing. For a while there, I was afraid you'd be mixed up in this, give the paper a black eye."

"Nice of you to be so thoughtful," I said.

"Never mind the sarcasm, Dempster. I already gave you a break—a big one. We can't keep your name out of the story, because you turned in the alarm. But we're killing the part about you being questioned, and we're not mentioning what you were up to, with the notebook." He paused. "You get it back?"

"I got it. So you needn't worry about the paper's reputation."

"Go to hell." Cronin paused. When he spoke again, his voice was calm. "Sure you're all right, Phil?"

"I'm all right. Just tired, that's all."

Another pause. And then, "Phil—you sure you haven't got anything more to tell me?"

"Quite sure. I leveled with Captain Dalton, gave him everything I know on it."

"All right. What are your plans now?"

"I'm hitting the sack. Tired. But I'll keep in touch with you."

"Do that."

"Right." I hung up. And then I did hit the sack, and the sack hit me, and I slept. Slept without dreams. Slept until it was dark.

I got up, took a bath, and thought about dinner. Almost dinner-time. Almost time to call—

She must have been sitting at the phone, waiting.

"Hello."

"Oh, it's you. Are you all right?"

"Yes, thanks."

"I called you this afternoon, from the office. Nobody answered."

"I was sleeping."

"Tired?"

"Not now. Hungry. You eaten yet?"

"No."

"I'll be around in fifteen minutes."

"Well—"

"Going to be coy?"

"Make it twenty. I've got to change my dress."

I gave her half an hour before I pulled up in front of the building on Fairhope. It was a former duplex, now converted to four apartments. My girl lived in the front upper.

My girl? Well—

She looked like my girl when she greeted me at the door. Tonight the dress was green, to match the eyes and set off the hair. It set off other things, to. On her, and inside me.

"You look good," she said. "A person would never think you'd been through—" A lip-biting pause. "I'm sorry."

"That's all right."

"Care for a drink?"

I shook my head. "Not drinking at the moment. Not smoking, either. Last night seems to have cured me of all my vices."

"Did it?"

"Well, most of them. But I'm still ready to eat."

"Fine. I'll get my hat. Where are we going?"

"I was thinking about the Chateau. Would you like that?"

"You should have told me. I'm not dressed for it."

"Sure you are. You look fine. And after being hauled out of bed that way—I'm sorry they dragged you into it."

"I'm not." Diana looked at me as if she meant it. "They thought you started the fire, didn't they?"

"Looks that way. But your alibi fixed things. Sweet of you."

"You needn't thank me. I only told them the truth."

"But—" I hesitated. "You didn't really leave me at one, you know."

"I thought I did. It must have been around one when I caught the bus. Maybe five or ten minutes earlier at the most, come to remember. Should I have told them it was any earlier?"

"You definitely shouldn't," I answered. "One o'clock was just dandy. Saved my life with your story. Honey, I could hug you."

I stepped forward with every intention in the world of doing just that.

Diana moved back, eyes widening.

"Phil," she whispered. "Are you saying what I think you're saying? Did *you* start that fire?"

"Of course not." I didn't like the way she moved back, but at least she was calling me "Phil," now. "As a matter of fact, there's nothing to show that anybody started it."

"Oh, but there is," she told me. "Haven't you seen the papers? The Fire Marshal made a statement this noon. They found out how it was set. Somebody must have crawled in through the basement window and dumped a gallon of kerosene over the coal-pile and the shed down there, and on the stairs, too. That's how those men were trapped upstairs—the flames came right up the stairwell."

"How could they tell?"

"I guess they found the empty tin tossed on the coal-pile. Something like that. Anyway, it's in the paper." She handed me the *Globe*. "Read it if you want to. I'll get my hat."

I read it. Cronin had done a good job. My name was mentioned, but only as a passerby who had turned in the alarm. The cab-driver's statement wasn't included at all.

Dalton didn't get much of a play, either. The

story was built around the Fire Marshal and the Chief of the Fire Department. Sure enough, they claimed arson. Various members and former members of the White Brotherhood were being held for questioning. Of course the Fire Marshal didn't actually come right out and *say* it was arson. His statement was full of "indications lead us to believe" and "apparently" and "it appears." But there was no doubt about it, now. And they were investigating.

I skipped over the second-page stories about the White Brotherhood and Amos Peabody. The whole story of the cult was there—the story I'd intended to write. Now my opportunity had gone. Gone up in smoke.

That part wasn't important. What was important was how the fire had started. It would be easy to crawl through an open cellar window and find a convenient can of kerosene lying around. Almost any basement contains something like that—if not kerosene, then oil or cleaning fluid or some old rags or wastepaper. Even wood would do. Wood and newspapers. There are a thousand ways to start a fire. And it could be done so swiftly, so very swiftly. Into the cellar, up the stairs, and out again, all in five or ten minutes. Five or ten minutes was plenty of time.

Thinking about it made me want to take a drink. But before I acted on the impulse, Diana walked back into the room. She had her hat on, carried her bag.

"Will I need my coat?" she asked.

"No. It's still quite warm. Almost like summer. I wish I had a convertible."

"This is luxury enough." She smiled. "The Chateau—I've never been there. How did you guess that's where I wanted to go?"

"Psychic," I said.

Only I wasn't. If I'd been psychic, I would have driven fifty miles in the opposite direction.

Oh, it looked fine when we came in, and the menu was fancy, the service exceptional, the food superb. But I couldn't eat anything. Not when I saw them come in with the shishkabob. The shishkabob, served to some godawful gourmets at the next table. The shishkabob, served on a flaming sword—

"What's the matter?"

I pointed. She stared at the flames, the blue and red flames. I looked away, across the room, just in time to see another waiter wheel a serving-cart on which rested *crepes suzette*.

"Does that disturb you?"

I shook my head. And I tried to believe it didn't. What was the matter with me, was I getting a persecution-complex? Maybe it was worse than that. Maybe it was a guilt-complex. Had to get hold of myself. Suppose somebody began to play *Smoke Gets in Your Eyes*. Was that any reason for me to get up and run?

"I'm all right," I said. And after a moment I was, but I still didn't feel like eating. The steak was good, very well-done, and a bit charred on one side. That's the way I liked it—charred.

Or did I?

The dinner was turning into an ordeal. And yet she was there, smiling at me, the copper curls like living flame—

Stop it!

I made myself talk, made myself ask her all the questions I wanted her to answer. And she did answer, but half the time I wasn't listening to what she said.

All I remember is that her folks lived in Ohio, she'd been born there, her mother was divorced and when she remarried Diana had come here to finish school. She worked as a secretary now for some doctor.

I pretended to pay attention, pretended to be interested. Ordinarily I would have been, but this wasn't ordinarily. This was red flames and blue flames and trying to remember where I'd been at five to, ten to, one, five after, ten after. No stains or dirt on my clothes, but why should there be? It didn't make sense, because I'm afraid of fire, afraid of fire—

Then we were having coffee and the waiter came around and started to light the candle at our table, and I stood up very quickly.

"Let's go," I said.

She looked at me, then rose. When we went out she slipped her arm through mine. "Poor Phil," she said. "So upset. Sure you couldn't use a drink?"

"Just one."

We stopped at the bar out in front, and I had just one. We were out of there in five minutes.

The night was warm, but I could feel a breeze off the lake.

"Come on," I said. "Let's take a little ride."

We took a little ride and we didn't talk much. Ended up down at the lake—not near the regular beach, but further up, in a little place I knew. We had to go down through the bushes to get there, but we made it. I carried a blanket from the car.

It was nice down there, and peaceful in the dark. I spread the blanket and we lay down. I'd told her not to be coy when I talked to her over the phone, and apparently the remark had been unnecessary. She wasn't the coy type.

She wasn't coy and she wasn't shy. I don't know what I expected when we went down there. She was probably the most attractive woman I'd ever met, but this was only the second time we'd been together, and I'm no thoroughbred wolf. I supposed maybe we could rest for a while, and talk, perhaps hold hands and kiss. That would satisfy me.

But she wasn't resting, and she wasn't talking. And it was her hand that sought mine, her lips that came to mine, not as an offering but as an onslaught. Her mouth was a moving hunger, meeting and mingling with my own. Her mouth moved, and her hands moved, and her body moved, and now I knew that this would not satisfy me. Then I was moving, and she was suddenly still, but this I did not realize until later. Much later, when I sat up and habit hurried my hand to my pocket, in search of a cigarette.

"I thought you didn't smoke any more," she whispered.

"You cured me," I said. "You cured me, Diana. Of a lot of things."

"I'm glad."

I lay beside her. "Are you? Really? I didn't hurt you or—"

"You can't hurt me, Phil. No one can hurt me, darling. Not any more."

I puffed. The red tip of the cigarette glowed like a beacon. A warning-beacon? I didn't know, but I couldn't halt my voice.

"What do you mean? Was there some man who tried to—"

She put her mouth against my chest and laughed at my heart. "Some man? Phil, I might as well be honest with you. There have been a lot of men. A lot."

"Tell me."

"Why should I?"

"You know damned well why."

"No, I don't."

"You want me to say it, do you?"

"Say what?"

"That I'm in love with you."

"Are you?"

"Can't you feel it? Did you think I'd—"

She was laughing again. "Of course I do. Any man would. You're all alike. There's only one thing you're after, and you'll say anything, do anything, to get it. And then you run away."

"I'm not running, Diana. I'm here. I want to stay here, with you." I took another puff, looking at the glowing end. "And you're being cynical when you say all men are alike. You know it's not true—admit it."

"My father was different," she murmured. "But he was the only one. And what good did it do him? My mother knew how he felt, and she didn't care. She took advantage of it, cheated on him. When I was a little girl, she used to bring the others to the house. She didn't care if I knew, didn't care if I saw her. She didn't care about him, either. And when she met the man she wanted, she got a divorce. *She* got it, and made him pay. And now she cheats on my step-father. But that's all right. He'd do it to her. He tried to get me, once, before I left home. That's why I went away."

I could feel her mouth working and twisting against my chest.

"Don't," I said. "It's all right. I'm not like that. You'll see."

"That's what they all say," she told me. "Oh don't worry, I'm not blaming you. You're a man. I can understand how you feel. But how could my mother feel that way? Like a man, I mean, really wanting to—"

The warmth of the evening suddenly seeped away and I felt cold. Diana seemed to be changing before my very eyes. She was becoming strange, and a stranger, twisting, melting—like in a movie I had once seen about a wax museum where there was a fire and the wax statues softened and the features ran together into monstrous shapes . . . I caught myself slipping into the Dream and forced my mind back to reality.

"But don't you want to?"

"No. I hate it." She sat up. "If you hadn't forced me—" .

"Forced you?" I took a long drag on my cigarette. "What are you talking about?"

"You know what I'm talking about, Phil."

"No I don't. All I know is that I love you, and I thought you felt the same way about me, you acted as if you did."

"That's a lie."

She was on her feet now, and I rose, tossing the cigarette away, tossing everything away because this wasn't reasonable, it didn't make sense.

"Take your filthy hands off me!"

Now my hands were filthy. Why? I hadn't done anything to her, and yet she hated me. I could see it in the way her eyes blazed. They were blazing into mine now, because I had grabbed her. I held her close.

She tried to break loose and I caught her wrists. They were like ice. Her entire body was stiff, frozen. She *was* ice.

She was ice, and suddenly *I* was fire. I was fire, my mouth matching hers, my kisses like showers of sparks kindling a flame, my hands incendiary, my body burning, consuming hers in consummation.

Fire—anger—passion—makes you see red. Copper hair against the blanket, billowing and burning and blazing. And her body a white flame, turning to a shivering scarlet. The fire was igniting the ice and that was crazy because ice doesn't burn.

But then it was all crazy, the way she turned red, the way everything turned red. It was all crazy, but it was *real.*

For I had lifted my head and I was seeing fire. Real fire, real flames. The brush was burning! The brush, where I'd tossed my cigarette—

Then I was rising and she was rising, and she stared at me and then at the blaze. Her eyes were open and her mouth was open, too, and the scream came from her eyes as well as from her throat.

The flames were like dancing devils, climbing up the slope. She turned and ran down the beach, then clambered along the bank. I stood there, trying to move, calling, "Diana! Come back—wait!"

She didn't come back and she didn't wait. I beat at the brush with the blanket, showered sand on the sparks and then stamped and trampled and crushed the burning branches with my frantic feet.

Then the fire was out. The fire was out, and she was gone.

I climbed the bluff, panting, too winded to call. It wouldn't have been any use. When I got to the top of the slope, where the car was, she had disappeared.

I gunned the engine, wheeled down the road. I thought maybe I'd catch up to her, but I didn't. She hadn't come this way. Then I found a path and turned around—went back in the other direction. It was only a few blocks to the main highway. I didn't see her anywhere along the route. She must have hitched a ride right away. Thumbed her way out of my life.

All at once I didn't care any more. Let her go. Diana Rideaux, with her twisted ideas about men and love. Just as well I'd found out when I did. You can't live with a person whose mind works like that. Full of crazy impulses, crazy notions.

But what about me, tossing that cigarette? Did I know what I was doing, subconsciously? Was I acting on a crazy impulse, a crazy notion? You can't live with a person whose mind works like that.

How was I going to live with myself?

I put the thought aside, lighted another cigarette. I didn't really want to smoke, but I forced myself to, just to prove something. To prove that it was all my imagination, to prove that it could happen to anyone. Brushfires start every day. Careless smokers, dropping matches and butts. Did they go around accusing themselves of being pyromaniacs because of an accident like that?

Driving along, I began to feel better. I felt good enough to switch on the car radio. The music was calming, soothing. At least, that's how it began. Then it began to shriek and blare and scream. And as it did so, I recognized it—recognized it, and nearly ripped the knob from the panel trying to shut it off.

Why, of all things, did they have to be playing *The Ritual Fire Dance?*

6

HE WAS standing in front of the apartment
when I drove up that evening, and at first I
thought he was a clown—his face was so white,
his eyes were so black, his lips were so red.
Then, when I parked, crossed the street, and
passed him under the light, I realized that the
little man was no buffoon. The masks of
Comedy and Tragedy are strangely alike. This
man's face was unnaturally pallid, his eyes
deep-set and circled with the straining stain of
fatigue. His lips were red because he'd bitten
them.

I stared at him as I prepared to open the hall
door, and he stared back.

"Looking for someone?" I asked.

"Just waiting, Brother."

I went inside, walked up to my door. Then I finally came to—came up out of the fog of fancy and fire and fear long enough to realize what he had said. *"Brother."* The little man was a cultist.

The key was already in the door, but I yanked it out. I turned and went down the stairs, out the door.

But the front walk was deserted now. The stranger with the bleeding lips was gone.

I looked down the street in both directions. No one was in sight. He'd vanished, God knows where or why. And what had he been waiting for?

Up the stairs, two at a time. I got the key out, opened the door, switched on the light. Then I breathed a bit easier.

Whoever he was, whatever he was, he hadn't been here. My place was undisturbed.

My place was undisturbed, but I wasn't.

There was too much I didn't understand. A fire, and then another fire. A girl who feared me, and another who feared me, too—myself.

And now, the little man with the pale face, who was just waiting outside my apartment. Of course, it could be a coincidence. Those things happen. The long arm of coincidence might have placed him there.

But the long arm of coincidence ended in a claw, and I felt it clutching at my throat. The Tabernacle had gone up in flames and the general idea seemed to be that it hadn't been that dry a summer for it to have gone up all on its own. Somebody had lit it; somebody had lent Amos Peabody a helping hand to his Final Reward—which I'm sure Amos would have willingly passed up right at this juncture. And I was something more than just an innocent bystander. One, I had been on the scene. And two, I was doing a series of articles on the cults. Maybe somebody didn't like the idea. Maybe right at that very moment somebody was mentally thinking of me as a chicken on a spit.

It wasn't very funny. When I fry bacon, the hot grease always spatters me. I used to do that trick of lighting wooden matches with my thumbnail but the burning matchhead would invariably scorch my hand. And when I smoke cigarettes, the lit tip frequently falls off and burns a hole in my pants.

I've got a grudge against life, I thought shakily. *I get burned up all too easily* . . . And that thought was anything but hilarious, too.

I went to the telephone and dialed Schwarm. I needed him now, needed him at once. Sure, it was late, but Schwarm would come. I could talk to him, reason things out. He'd know. Schwarm always knew.

Dr. Milton Schwarm. They called him a psychiatrist, and he was good enough to be consultant for the police department on occasion. But I didn't think of him as a head-shrinker. For six months now he'd been my friend. He knew something about my problems, but I hadn't been able really to tell him everything. Hadn't wanted to, because he was my friend; I hated to change that for a professional relationship.

Right now, though, I was willing. More than willing. As I sat there, listening to the buzzing, I was eager.

Then the voice came.

"Hello," I said. "This is Phil Dempster. Is Doctor Schwarm there, please?"

"I'm sorry, Mr. Dempster. He's out of the city."

"Oh. When will he be back?"

"Friday evening, I believe."

"Thank you." I cradled the phone.

He'd be back Friday evening and this was only Wednesday. Two days. So much could happen before then.

But nothing was going to happen. I was just edgy, from not drinking. That's what comes when you lay off the fire-water.

Fire-water. Did I really think of it in that way?

Schwarm would know. I could tell him and he could tell me. But not now. Friday evening.

Now I had to sleep. And tomorrow there was a job to do. The Church of the Golden Atom. Professor Ricardi.

I dragged myself over to the couch, dragged out the notebook, and read about Professor Ricardi and his Golden Atoms. It was hard going, because I kept looking over my shoulder, kept jerking upright whenever I heard a noise from outside.

Eventually, though, I dozed off. Dozed off right there on the couch. When I woke up the sun was shining. Wednesday night had passed.

Curiously enough, I felt better. A shave and a shower helped still more. By the time I finished breakfast I was completely alert and ready to go to work.

I went to work.

Research is a slow business, but rewarding. I knocked off about five, after completing my rounds. My last stop was the *Globe* morgue, where I'd been digging through newspaper files on Professor Ricardi. I stopped in to see Ed Cronin, but he'd left, so I ate dinner alone.

This time I ate in a restaurant. Tonight wasn't going to be a repetition of Tuesday evening. I drove out to Grace Boulevard in plenty of time, and parked right in front of the Church of the Golden Atom.

This was no converted meeting-hall. A trim, modern brick building in a substantial residential neighborhood, with a blazing yellow neon sign projecting from one corner: CHURCH OF THE GOLDEN ATOM.

Respectable, I thought. You couldn't have told it from some of the other churches in the neighborhood. They probably had dances and Bingo on Saturday nights and a young people's club and were charter members of the neighborhood business association.

Something about the sight of the sign made me hesitate. It was so bright. I didn't want to walk under it, and then I knew why, and I told myself *the sign blazes, but the building won't burn.*

After that I could go inside.

The outer hall was already crowded. They were all here tonight—the middle-aged widows in the clutches of the climacteric, the pale young men who avoided your eyes, the man with the shaggy eyebrows who kept mumbling to himself or an invisible companion, the girl with the goiter, the old woman with the bright orange hair. I recognized the types. The comfortable middle-class, when it begins to crack up around the edges and lose its faith in the usual faiths. Salvation begins to mean more and more to them, and they don't want to wait for it after death—they want it now.

And there were others I took special pains to observe; others *with* special pains. The lame, the halt and the blind. Canes tapped, crutches clumped, wheel-chairs rolled.

I passed a table bearing books and literature. THE GOLDEN KEY was the title stamped on the bright blue binding of the book. The magazine was called ATOMIC SCIENCE, and the smaller tracts were no less imposing in their headings.

A fat woman sat behind the table, breathing benevolence and Sen-Sen. At her right was a tin box, and at her left, a half-filled bottle of coke.

"Can I help you?" she asked.

I nodded and passed on. Another table loomed ahead. This layout was presided over by an elderly gentleman who wore a hearing aid. A gaudy chart stood propped before him, and next to it was a pyramid of 5-ounce jars, each bearing a gold label reading VITAL CREAM. Marching down the side of the table were smaller glass containers. The gold label on these identified them as ATOMIC ENERGY CAPSULES.

"Yes sir?" said the elderly man.

I hesitated for a moment, then fished in my pocket. "Better give me one of each," I said. "How much?"

"That'll be six dollars for the cream and five for the capsules," he told me.

I said something under my breath which I hoped his hearing aid wouldn't pick up. But I gave him the money. It would be worthwhile to get this stuff analyzed by a pharmaceutical chemist.

Then, on second thought, I went back and bought a copy of THE GOLDEN KEY for five dollars and two issues of ATOMIC SCIENCE at fifty cents each.

Seventeen dollars for research, so far. Not a bad deal for Professor Ricardi.

No, Professor Ricardi did all right. I found that out when I went inside. His church setup was conventional enough—rows of pews on either side of a center aisle, leading down to the rostrum and the altar. The usual organ was being manned by the usual organist, who played the usual music.

Behind the altar was the banner; a huge,

golden sun emitting a corona of gilt-and-rhinestone sparks. In front of the altar, a moment after I entered, was the eminent Professor Ricardi himself.

He glittered.

His robe was golden, and so was his hair, and his beard, and the rings on his long, slim fingers that rose to invoke a benediction upon the congregation.

His voice was golden, too. And it was of gold that he spoke. Not the crass, coarse gold of material riches, but the true gold of the Spirit. Nature's gold. Here was a treasure without end, lavished upon us all, by the Primal Atom which was Being.

All Life springs from the Atom. The Atom is the source of creation, the father of us all. What is the biblical "Adam" but a misreading of "Atom"?

The earth was born from the atomic energy of the sun. The sun—the Prime Atom—is the source of all Life. Solar energy rules the earth, and from it we can tap untold blessings if we possess the key.

Yet woe unto those wicked ones who deny the truth, who seek to harness the Atom to their own evil ends! Those who tamper with Prime Matter, who divide the Atom and release its Essence are cursed—they will bring down doom and destruction upon themselves.

They had best turn to the Church before too late; learn the Truth as set forth in ATOMIC SCIENCE and THE GOLDEN KEY. There all can find eternal Youth, eternal Health, eternal Life—yes, and riches and power too, for those who desire such trifles.

As for Professor Ricardi, he was above these petty needs. His years of labor as a Cosmic Scientist in the secret laboratories of Tibet had borne sufficient reward when he discovered the shining truth of what he sought.

For forty years he had journeyed through the Wilderness of Error before he found the Way. Then a few chance words let slip to jealous fellow-scientists had resulted in their discovery of the Truth, and their misuse of it to produce the Atomic Bomb.

Now, with such power in the hands of the forces of Evil, Professor Ricardi had determined to step forward and lead the world to the Truth. Time was short, and it would be a close race between Destruction and Construction. But he was ready.

Professor Ricardi had dedicated his eternal existence to delivering the message of the Golden Atom, to dispensing Nature's Own Source of Life—pure sunlight—in the form of ATOMIC CAPSULES and VITAL CREAM. These scientifically prepared aids to immortality were augmented by the Inner Light of Truth shining in the pages of THE GOLDEN KEY.

So said Professor Ricardi, for almost an hour. From time to time his pronouncements were punctuated and accented by the organ.

And then the light dimmed, and he offered

up a prayer to the Atomic Power Who Rules All Being, and the choir rose and chanted.

The Power descended on Ricardi, haloing his golden head. And he raised his hands to draw unto himself all those who believed, who could feel the Atomic Energy flowing from him into their bodies to heal and to save. He called upon them to surrender to the Power, to let the injured atoms rearrange themselves in perfect harmony.

It was the ultimate in phoniness. The cheap pitch was as obvious as the peroxide rinse on his hair and beard. The organ came in like a soap-opera cue, and the halo was a spotlight operated by a union electrician.

But Professor Ricardi held out his hands, and they came. They came to the altar, creeping and crawling and tottering.

All eyes were on the altar, now, as Professor Ricardi prayed over the afflicted. They were filing past him one by one. He held their hands, gazed into their eyes, and prayed. The crowd watched—and I watched the crowd.

There was a fat man sitting on my left. He stared at the altar, twisting the brim of his hat as he watched. On my right, a girl began to sob convulsively. Professor Ricardi had them now, held them in the palm of his hand.

The hand went out, touching an old man's forehead. He stood there, head bowed for a moment. Then the head jerked upright and the man straightened—straightened, and let his crutches clatter to the floor.

From either side of me came gasps and moans.

Now Ricardi bent over a woman in a wheelchair. Again he pressed his fingers against her temples. Suddenly the woman shrieked and rose from the chair. She rose and walked, and the crowd made an ancient sound.

Ricardi stepped back, smiling and shaken, as the tumult rose. Then the organ came up suddenly, the lights were on, and a grey-haired acolyte was on the platform, pleading for a Free-Will Offering. Ushers ran down the aisles.

The fat man on my left reached into his pocket and came up with a ten-dollar bill. The girl on my right fished three dollars and some change from her purse. The room resounded with the clink of coins, the tonguing tumult of those who had been privileged to witness wonders.

I'd seen enough. I rose and tried to move down the aisle toward the platform, toward the man who'd tossed aside his crutches and the woman who rose from her wheelchair to walk again.

But the crowd milled and blocked my way, breathing and babbling all around me. I fought through phrases, brushed past bodies, edged excitement at every step.

And when I reached the platform, both the man and the woman were gone. Ricardi had disappeared, too. I tried to catch the eye of the grey-haired acolyte, but he was surrounded by ushers. They were emptying their collections into a tin box.

I turned to retrace my steps up the aisle. Maybe they'd slipped out a side entrance. I might still overtake them if I got out in time.

The crowd barred my path but I pushed on. Pushed on to the edge of the lobby, where yet other groups clustered around the tables, buying THE GOLDEN KEY and ATOMIC ENERGY CAPSULES. I kept searching for a sight of the three faces I sought.

I caught a glimpse of a back bobbing in the doorway ahead. Somebody was standing there, and even at a distance I knew that I was being surveyed. As I stared, the short man turned to face me fully, and I recognized him. For an instant I saw the white face, the black eyes, the red lips of the clown. Then he disappeared in the street beyond.

He'd been here tonight, watching me. *Why?*

Ricardi and the others could wait. I had to find out about this, first. Slowly I burrowed my way through the lobby, fighting towards the freedom of the doorway beyond.

Just as I reached it, the hand came out and tugged at my shoulder.

"Phil—wait a minute!"

I turned and gazed into the smiling moon-face of Doctor Milton Schwarm.

7

WE SAT over coffee in the restaurant down the street.

"But they told me you were out of town," I said. "I never expected to run into you here—and on the same errand."

Schwarm shook his head. "It isn't the same. You're out after a newspaper feature. Mine is a clinical investigation. As I told you, one of my patients was formerly a member of the Golden Atom sect. I wanted to get a line on the organization for that reason. And on this Professor Ricardi. These so-called cures are an interesting phenomenon. If I could find a reasonable excuse, I'd like to interview the man and the woman we saw tonight. Perfectly classical examples of hysterical—"

"Wrong," I interrupted. "They were plants. Fakes, I'm sure of it. Just as sure as I know Professor Ricardi isn't a Professor."

"What makes you so certain?"

I pulled out the notebook. "I didn't walk in there cold. Did some snooping around first. You want to know what I found out?"

"If it's not confidential."

"You'll see most of it in the *Globe* a week from Sunday. Might as well get the facts now."

"Go ahead." Schwarm leaned back and picked up his coffee-cup.

I scanned my jottings. "Your friend Professor Ricardi has a very conventional history. His real name is Joseph Edward Clutt. Born in Spokane, in 1929. Father was a plumber. Joe was an apprentice until he ran away with a medicine show.

"He came to town here in 1951, and was rejected by the draft because of narcotic addiction. In 1956 he was named correspondent in a divorce action brought against Mrs. Agatha Loodens by her husband, Frederick. Apparently he had offered her more than the usual plumbing services."

Schwarm put his cup down. "You mean he was still a plumber in 1956? What about those trips to the Orient and Tibet?"

I grinned. "The nearest Joe Clutt ever came to the Orient was an opium pad in 'Frisco."

"Go ahead," Schwarm said. "This is interesting. I've always wondered how a cult was born."

"Simple. Shortly after the divorce, Mrs. Loodens' former husband passed away. He left her a small pharmaceutical supply business. It had government contracts during the Korean war, but it was in bad shape by '58.

"Her lover, Joe Clutt, took over. It was he who continued the manufacture of what has since become ATOMIC ENERGY CAPSULES and VITAL CREAM. The idea of the cult came from there."

"You mean this plumber dreamed up the whole procedure in order to sell his product?"

"Not quite. There's a third party involved. Their business attorney, a man named Weatherbee. I'm pretty certain the basic notion came from him. He could easily have written THE GOLDEN KEY and coached Joe Clutt in his new role. Clutt had a medicine-show and carnival background, remember, and no doubt he possessed a certain amount of personal magnetism. At least the late Mr. Loodens thought so.

"But Weatherbee and Mrs. Loodens are the brains. They got him to dye his hair, change his name, taught him the catch-phrases, and invested money in printing up the books and packaging the merchandise.

"They opened headquarters, and probably used their social and business connections to spread the word and attract the early converts. And the racket caught on. They're making a fortune in daily lessons, private courses, personality-readings. The books are going out by mail-order as well as through the Church itself. The pills and the cream sell that way too. And by far the biggest percentage of profit must come from the contributions and the Free-Will Offerings. I understand they plan to open a branch in Chicago soon."

"You wouldn't believe people would be so gullible," Schwarm murmured. "A personal observation," he hastened. "Not a professional one."

I snorted. "They don't believe it because they've been convinced of anything—cultists believe because they want to believe. Five years ago I went to a pseudo-seance and I've never forgotten it. There must have been a couple of hundred cultists present in the hall. A lot of middle-aged people but a lot of young ones, too—teenagers and married couples who'd lugged their kids along. The medium was a skinny little guy about fifty who needed a clean shirt and a shave and a bath. His wife was a fat, frowzy old witch who sold tickets and booklets and did the opening spiel about how her husband would go into a trance and communicate with the Great Ones in the Beyond.

"On cue the little guy closed his eyes, worked up a sweat, then started spouting gibberish in a high, sing-song voice. I recognized a few words of Spanish and I suspect most of the rest of it was Chinese. His wife 'translated' on how the Great One was pleased to be called from Beyond the Veil and gave a few predictions as to what was coming in the future and then gave stereotyped answers to stereotyped questions from the audience. The act wouldn't have fooled a ten-year-old but the people there were literally on the edge of their seat. During the intermission a friend of mine made snide remarks and we were nearly mobbed. The light of truth isn't exactly what these people are looking for."

Schwarm lit a cigarette. "But how do they get away with it?" he asked. "What about the authorities? Don't they know this man isn't a professor, that he's running a phoney religious racket?"

"Please," I said. "You're supposed to be a psychiatrist. *Naiveté* doesn't become you. Clutt is Ricardi—his change of name was legalized three years ago. He is also a professor, and if he wanted to he could call himself a doctor, too. Anybody can get a degree in metaphysics if he's willing to pay the dough to one of the mail-order schools. And your use of the term 'phoney religious racket' is open to question. You know all sects and cults are tolerated, providing their leaders don't indulge in fortune-telling." I shrugged. "However, my article may get a few people to thinking."

"Perhaps." Schwarm put his cigarette down. I couldn't help but watch. I was watching everything that burned these days. "But since when have you had this sudden interest in crusading? I thought you were writing another book."

"I put it aside for a few weeks. It went stale on me."

"What seemed to be the trouble?"

He asked the question casually, but I knew Schwarm well enough to realize he was serious. Here was my opportunity to tell him—tell him everything. About Diana, and the fire at the White Brotherhood tabernacle, and my drinking before that fire, and the reasons for my drinking. But there would be no backing out if I got that far. Behind the fire was the drinking and behind the drinking was the dream, and behind the dream was something I couldn't talk about.

I *wanted* to, but I *couldn't*. Because of what he might say. He was a psychiatrist, and he'd be able to tell me what was wrong, and I was afraid of hearing it.

So I just shook my head and said, "Guess I ran out of ideas. Too much introspection. This little assignment gives me a chance to get out, get away from myself for a while."

"Get away from yourself, eh?"

"Please." I smiled at him. "No bedside manner."

"Sorry. But you know, Phil, anytime you feel that you have a problem you'd like to talk over—"

"Sure," I said. "I know. And thanks." I glanced at my watch. "Got to run along now. It's late. Can I drop you off?"

"No, I've got my car." He stood up, stubbing out his cigarette in the ashtray. A few sparks still smouldered. I glanced around the restaurant. Suppose one of those sparks blew out of the ashtray and lodged against the drapes there on the wall? If the drapes caught fire they'd burn quickly, and the walls were wood, they would burn, and the whole place could go up in flames—

Schwarm walked down the aisle and I quickly extinguished the smouldering butt. It was foolish, but I couldn't help it. Suppose he saw me? What could I say, "I'm a Boy Scout and this is Fire Prevention Week"?

But he didn't see me, nobody saw me, and everything was all right. Schwarm paid for my coffee, we went outside, and said goodbye on the street.

"Call me for lunch one of these days," he said. "Let's have a visit."

"Will do."

I watched him as he climbed into his car and drove away. Then I turned and started down the block toward my own parking-place.

It was dark in the middle of the block here on the sidestreet, but not too dark to make out the figure that leaned against the side of the car. And even in the dimness I saw and recognized that white face—the clown-face.

He stood up when he saw me.

"I've been waiting, Brother," he said.

"Yes. So I see."

"I wanted to make sure you were alone." He peered up at me, teeth protruding over the bitten lips. "You *are* alone, aren't you?"

91

I nodded. I was alone, and didn't like it. Alone on a dark sidestreet with a fanatic who had waited for me.

"That is good. Otherwise I would not take you. I had to be sure."

"Sure of what?" *Sure that I was alone so he could kill me?*

He was standing quite close, and suddenly his hand came out of his coat. It didn't come out alone. I caught the gleam of the knife-blade, and before I could move the point pressed in my side.

"Be very still," he murmured. "I must make doubly certain." His right hand held the knife against me. His left hand went to my coat, opened it. His cold fingers crawled across my chest, unbuttoning my shirt.

My hands went up, and the knife dug in. "Don't try that," he whispered. "I will not harm you, I seek a sign."

Crazier than hell. This was crazier than hell, he was crazier than hell, I was—

His icy fingers raised gooseflesh on my breast as he lifted my T-shirt. For a moment he peered down at my chest. His hand pressed it.

"Good," he said. "It is as I hoped. You are not one of them. There is no mark."

"What mark?"

"The mark of the Beast. The mark of the Evil One. You are not one of them after all. You are pure. So you will help me." His hand left me. I buttoned my shirt and coat.

"Help you how? Who are you, anyway?"

"I am the one chosen. Chosen for vengeance."

What do you say when you hear a thing like that? You can't come out with, "Make sense"— not when the sharp edge of a knife is still within slicing distance of your stomach. I stared down into the white clown-face and waited.

"You will help me," he repeated. "Come." He nudged me in the direction of the car. "Get in. I'll tell you how to go."

"Where are we going?" I asked—but I got in the car while I spoke, because the knife nudged.

"To issue warning."

"The police?"

"They are enemies. You know that, surely. They hate the Brotherhood."

"Brotherhood? Are you from the White Brotherhood? Is that where you're taking me?"

"The Brotherhood has ended in the Fire of Wrath. You know that. And the Fire of Wrath will consume all before it unless others are warned in time."

Little clown-face with the knife, whispering to me in the darkness. I shuddered, moving away across the front seat. His eyes and his knife followed me.

"We must go now. Hurry. It's 1902 Benson Street."

The address meant nothing to me—Benson Street was way on the other end of town, in the suburbs.

"Who's there?"

"The one we warn. Quickly, now."

I drove. I drove, hoping we'd pass a squad

car so that I could be picked up for speeding. I drove, hoping for a break, a blowout, a freak accident, anything.

But there was no hope. There was only the darkness of the streets, the darkness beside me, and the little man with the big knife. I drove him, but he was driving me. Driving me into darkness and—?

"Faster," he murmured. "We may be too late. The Fire of Wrath moves swiftly to consume the world, for the Day of Doom is at hand—"

"Fire," I said. "You keep talking about fire. Did you burn down the Brotherhood tabernacle?"

The knife bit into my side, and the sweat poured out as I waited for his hand to move, waited for the car to strike a rut. I was an inch away from eternity—just a single, cold steel inch.

But the knife moved no further. "I will not kill you, Brother, because I understand. You do not know."

"Why don't you tell me, then?"

"You shall hear, in a few moments. When I tell *him*. I want you both to hear."

"Is that why you're taking me out to this place instead of going yourself?"

"Yes. If I went alone, he would not listen. He would say that I was loony. You know what 'loony' means, Brother?"

I was afraid to answer that one in any way. I drove silently, turning off Ammon Boulevard onto Benson Street.

The voice was strident in my ear, now. " 'Loony' means crazy. That's what it means, Brother. Crazy in the head. They used to say that about me when I was little. Before I joined the Brotherhood. The Reverend knew I wasn't loony, though, and he believed in the Voices. But some of the others still called me that. It makes me mad. It makes me feel like taking my knife and cutting out their tongues. Their tongues that lie and lie."

I sat there, silent and sweating, driving down Benson and watching the houses thinning out as we reached the hillside area of the suburb. Now we were climbing, and he was whispering. "But you'll know in a minute. And he'll know, too. Know that I'm not loony, that I'm telling the truth about the Fire of Wrath. He must know, because he's the next, the next on the list—"

The trees were thick on either side now, and the 1900 block was just around the next sharp turn. We made it. 1902 was the big house on the right-hand side, set back on the steep driveway.

I drove in. "Here we are," I said.

The house was dark and silent. As we climbed out of the car I fancied I could see a dim light burning on the second floor, through a rear window.

We went to the front door. "Whom do I ask for?" I muttered. "What do I say? Busting in on somebody at this hour of the night—"

"I'll do the talking," said the little man with the knife. "Just hurry."

I rang the bell. Waited. Rang again.

"You see?" I turned to him. "Nobody home. Or else they're sound asleep."

The little man pushed me aside. He began to hammer on the door with the butt of the knife.

"No use," I told him. I started to turn away. He reached for me.

"There must be," he said. "Look at the light."

I stepped back and gazed up at the window again. There was a light burning there, burning more brightly than before.

Burning *too* brightly—

I turned to him and saw that he already knew. He could see the flame, smell the smoke now.

"Down to the corner," I said. "Turn in an alarm."

"What are you going to do?"

"Got to get inside."

"Don't—it's too late—no use now. You'll be killed—"

Now it was his turn to tremble. I looked at the little clown-face and suddenly I wasn't afraid any more. Before there was time to think it over, I'd reached out and grabbed the knife.

"Where are you going with that?"

"I'll show you." No sense trying the door. I walked over to the French window off the porch facing the walk. I shattered the glass around the outside lock with the butt of the knife. The window gave.

A suffocating wave of mingled heat and smoke poured out.

"Hurry!" I yelled. "Get that alarm turned in."

Without waiting any longer, I stepped into the room. It was dark, and the smoke stung my eyes and nostrils. There was nothing I could do about my eyes, but I groped for a handkerchief to hold over my nose and mouth.

Then I moved across the room, following the wall. I almost tripped over a floor-lamp, and I bruised my knee against a sofa. But I reached the hall, felt for a light switch, then realized I wouldn't need it.

The hall was light enough, now. I could see the flickering flare from upstairs; it was like a beacon to guide me. Or to warn me.

The smoke was thick, acrid. The stench was sickening. And the fire was upstairs, I didn't want to go up there, I was afraid of fire—

But I went. I was afraid of fire, but I was more afraid of myself. I had to go. Maybe the answer was upstairs, maybe I'd learn the secret.

I took the stairs two at a time. As I rounded the curve, the stench and the smoke and the heat seemed to coalesce, forming an invisible hand; a big, hot hand that tried to push me back.

I half-turned on the stairway, choking and gasping. The hand was pushing me down, and

I wanted to shrink away from it. But the blaze beckoned above. I faced the hand again, ducked, and slipped through the invisible fingers.

Then I was on the upper landing, and the smoke swirled all about me. The hall was black with it. The rug was smouldering in the hall, and there were little tongues of flame licking and nibbling and eating.

From the room at the end of the corridor came other tongues. And the smoke poured out in a choking cloud. I stumbled toward the open doorway. The heat was rising, and I could scarcely see. I stood there blinking, trying to look into the bedroom. A burst of smoke, a burst of flame, another burst of smoke—but I caught glimpses between: Glimpses of Inferno.

Somebody had set fire to the curtains. Somebody had set fire to the drapes. Somebody had torn the bedclothes off the bed and piled them in a great heap at the foot, to smoulder and burn. They were cloth and gave off a suffocating odor, but they were burning more briskly now. In a moment or so the bed would catch fire—and somebody wanted that to happen.

Whoever had set the blaze and stripped the bedding had also left a single sheet for another purpose. This sheet had been torn to long shreds and used for tying the arms and legs of the man who lay on the bed—lay face down, head almost lost to view in the rising smoke.

He wasn't struggling, wasn't even moving now. I could understand why. That smoke was enough to asphyxiate anyone.

It had been planned this way. First, asphyxiation and in a few moments now, incineration. The heat seared my hands and forehead. The wallpaper had curled and burned, and the fire ran along the floorboards.

I ran over to the bed, kicking the burning shag-rug aside. I bent down, took hold of the bound man's waist. No time to free his hands or feet. We had to get out of here, fast.

I lifted, hoisting him over my shoulder. He hung like a sack. A heavy sack, a heavy burden to carry back down through the smoke-shrouded hall, the smouldering stairway.

Coughing, wheezing, choking. Groping, staggering, almost falling. Panting, trembling, shuddering as a sudden flash of flame licked out from the window-curtains half-way down the stairs and seared my temple.

I thought I could hear shouts and the sound of sirens, but there was no way of being sure—not with the crackling and murmur that followed me down the stairs.

The room was just ahead, and beyond it was the window, and beyond the window was air. That's what I needed. Fresh air, cool air, a chance to put my burden down, a chance to lay down for a moment myself; lay down where I'd be safe from the flames.

Just a few steps more, now. And now I could see beyond into the street. The engines were arriving. I tried to find the little clown-faced man, but he was gone.

It didn't matter. What mattered was that I

was out at last, out in the open. I was safe. I could put him down now.

So I put him down. Put him down on his back, so I could see his face. Then I knew I wasn't safe any more, wasn't safe from the flames or what lurked behind them.

I was staring down at the face of Joseph Clutt, alias Professor Ricardi; the purple, strangulated countenance of the leader of the Golden Atom.

For a moment I stared, and then the face started to rush up toward me. No, it didn't rush up—I was going down. Going down into the fire and past the fire into darkness.

8

I THINK IT WAS Pythagoras who put forth a theory about eternal recurrence—the idea that the same things happen over and over again.

I wonder what Pythagoras would have thought if he'd been sitting in that little room, looking out of the window and watching the sunrise.

Actually, I didn't really care what he'd think. I only wished that he, or somebody else, would be here instead of myself. Sitting here just two days after the first time, and listening to Captain Dalton say, "It looks bad. You have to admit that. It looks bad."

"I admit nothing," I answered. "I've told you all I know about it. Why don't you pick up the little white-faced guy? And Schwarm?"

"We're looking for your mysterious kook

right now," Dalton replied. "And Doctor Schwarm is on his way over."

I hoped he'd get here quickly. I was tired of having that pipe point at me. Dalton managed to do it even when he glanced down and looked over his notes.

"You still insist you never had anything to do with Professor Ricardi," he said.

"I don't insist. I'm only telling you. I never saw the man until the meeting tonight."

"And this weirdo you claim you saw—"

"It's not a claim. I saw him, he was there, he stuck a knife in my ribs."

"All right." Dalton brushed his hand through his hair. "I'm going to talk to Ricardi's attorney now—this man Weatherbee. And Mrs. Loodens. Maybe they've got something to say that makes sense."

He left me sitting there wondering what they or anyone could say that would make sense. Oddly enough, though, I didn't feel too bad. Not then. Because I knew this was one fire I had nothing to do with—and I hadn't been afraid. Or had I? Even so, I'd gone in and tried to save Ricardi. I'd behaved normally, and that proved I *was* normal. Maybe.

But somebody was responsible. Somewhere there must be a firebug, a firebug; a tiger, tiger, burning bright—

What kind of creature had fastened itself on Ricardi, tied him down and left him to the flames?

I thought over possibilities. Diana Rideaux of

course. But she was ice, not fire. And she'd been with me the first time, she'd been with me the second time at the beach when my cigarette kindled the brush. Then she ran away. Copper-colored moth that feared flames. Not the right sort of animal at all.

What about the clown-faced man? He could have started the first one, yes, but if so then why was he afraid of his "enemies"? Why did he want to "warn" Ricardi? Surely he couldn't have tied Ricardi up, set the fire, then come clear across town and found me, brought me back. The blaze hadn't been going that long. Besides, even for a kook, such activity was incredible.

Still, he seemed to know Ricardi was next. How could that be? And why did he connect *me* with all this?

Somewhere, somehow, there was a pattern. They'd have to find him, make him talk. He didn't actually commit arson, but he must know who did. Where there's smoke, there's—

Schwarm came in.

"Come on," he said. "Let's get out of here, Phil."

"You talked to Captain Dalton?"

"That's right. Told him you were with me. Everything's cleared up."

"The hell it is. Never saw a worse mess in my life. You know what happened?"

"Yes." He held the door open for me. "But we can talk about that later."

This time they'd brought my car downtown.

103

I signed for it at the police garage. Schwarm waited for me.

"Can I drop you off somewhere?" I asked.

"At my office. Will you stop in for a minute?"

"I'm pretty tired."

"I know. But I thought we might talk this thing out. As a matter of fact, I promised Captain Dalton."

"You're on this case now?"

"Unofficially, yes. They call me in for consultation from time to time, as you know. Whenever something comes up which involves the suspicion of mental disorder."

"In other words, Dalton thinks I'm nuts. Is that it?"

"No. But—"

"You're a lousy psychiatrist," I said. "At least you might have figured out a way to humor me, kid me along."

Schwarm chuckled. "Maybe. Then again, perhaps I'm a pretty good man. At least, my apparently clumsy approach is working. I'm getting you to come up to my office on the strength of it, just because you resent the implication. Right?"

"You win," I said.

I drove him over to the Soames Building and parked in his parking space in the lot. It was still early morning, and his office was deserted. No receptionist; just the two of us, alone.

"Sit down and tell me all about it," Schwarm said. "Cigarette?"

"No, thanks." I had trouble speaking. My

throat was dry with thirst and something else. Fear. "Is this official?" I asked.

"I'm going to make notes, yes. But I'll respect your confidences, Phil."

"Sure." I leaned back in my chair. "Where should I start?"

"At the beginning."

"You mean last night, or the other night? You heard how I turned in the alarm for the White Brotherhood fire, I suppose?"

He nodded. "Yes. If that's the beginning, start there. *You* know where to start."

I knew, but I didn't want to tell. I couldn't tell. Not about the beginning, or the dream. And if I told him about wandering around in a daze, he'd pounce on that. *Be careful*, I reminded myself. *You must be very careful.*

So I repeated what I'd given Dalton when I made my statement. The story of meeting Diana Rideaux, going home, returning to the tavern for my notes. Then I went on from there, telling him what had happened after they picked me up and let me go again. Before I could help it, I'd gotten into the part where I saw Diana again and we went to the beach.

It was too late to stop, now. I had to go through with it, even though I realized my mistake. I gave him the story of the cigarette butt and the brush fire.

I kept looking at him as I spoke, but his face told me nothing. He was taking notes, all right, and that was all. For a moment I thought of explaining how the brush fire was an accident, and then I caught myself in time. If I protested, it would just arouse his suspicion. So I went on from there, to last night. I told about the Church of the Golden Atom meeting just as if he hadn't seen me there—about the restaurant and my encounter with the little clown-faced man outside. About the drive, and the fire, and finding Ricardi's body.

"There it is," I said. "You're interviewing the wrong guy, you know that now, don't you? If we had this weirdo character here, he could tell you what you want to find out."

"Perhaps." Schwarm put down his pencil. "But we must be practical. Your little friend isn't here, so we'll just work with what we've got."

"I can't tell you any more," I said. "You've had it."

"You've been very cooperative, Phil." He tapped the notes. "Your story is remarkably detailed. You have a good memory for facts."

"Got to, when you write for a living."

"But it occurs to me that you've omitted discussing one rather important angle in your story."

"What's that?"

"Nowhere in your account did you happen to mention just how you *felt* about these things. You didn't give me your reactions to all this."

"Why—" I shrugged. "I thought it was facts you were after. My feelings aren't important."

"Well, just for the sake of curiosity, then—

suppose you tell me what went on in your mind during these past three days."

"I was scared," I said. "Scared as hell. Who wouldn't be? Turn in an alarm and they pick you up and accuse you of being a firebug. Then this little off-beat character started to trail me. That wasn't exactly a picnic, either. And this girl—the way she acted, you'd think I'd been trying to rape her. Right after that came the brush-fire. That part really worried me."

"Why?"

I was in too deep to stop, now. "Because I wondered if it *was* an accident. I'm not entirely ignorant of your racket, you know. I've heard about the workings of the subconscious. When I tossed away that butt, I might have been acting on a concealed impulse to start a fire. In other words, seeing the first fire might have triggered me into deciding to set one myself. Maybe we're all potential pyromaniacs at heart."

"Is that what you think?"

"You're the doctor, you tell me."

Schwarm smiled. "Do you still feel that you might have had an impulse to fire the brush?"

"Not any more." I saw a way out, and I took it now. "Because of last night. I know I had nothing to do with Ricardi's death, and so do you. And when I went in to get him, I was just plain scared, again. Afraid of fire."

"But you went in."

"I had to."

"You could have waited for the firemen."

"A person doesn't think at a time like that," I answered. "The subconscious takes over."

"Then your subconscious dictated that you go into the burning building."

"Well—"

"And yet, consciously, you say you're afraid of fire."

"I—" Then I was on my feet. "No use, Doc. I can't explain it. I can't tell you any more."

"All right. I believe you. *You* can't. But perhaps this so-called subconscious of yours can. Are you willing to try?"

I had to nod. But I was beginning to sweat, now. "What are you going to do, hypnotize me? You want me to take one of those truth-drugs?"

Schwarm smiled. "Let's not be melodramatic, Phil. I don't use such methods in ordinary procedure. And while we're at it, I might as well add to your education. This 'subconscious' of yours is a rather outmoded concept. In my opinion, there is no area or entity, physical or psychic, which can be identified as a 'subconscious mind.' There is only a consciousness which receives and identifies all data. Some of this data is unpleasant. It is repressed, or even suppressed. But it has been received, and it's there; available in one form or another. Sometimes as fantasy, sometimes as symbolism—yet always it remains present and available for communication even in a distorted form. The fantasy content is a clue to the reality. The mind *tries* to communicate. Do you follow me?"

"Not completely."

"You will."

He went over to the files, came back with a bulky folder.

"What's that?"

"The method I use to discover clues. You've probably heard of it. The Rorschach test. Ink-blot cards. You look them over, tell me what the blots suggest. Nothing to it."

He was right. There was nothing to it. I gazed at the cards as he flashed them in turn, and he recorded my reactions. Some of the cards were red, some were red and orange, some red and orange and blue and green.

We went over them once in sequence. Then again, in a different order. Then a third time, in sequence. He asked for comments. I gave them. I didn't try to evade or avoid what came up.

Schwarm made notes. He put the cards away and sat back, reading. From time to time he came across a statement that prompted a question. I answered everything.

Finally he sat back and pushed the notes away.

"Well," I said. "What's the verdict? Am I a firebug?"

He smiled. "You answered that question yourself, a while back. Didn't you say you believed maybe we're all potential pyromaniacs at heart?"

"That was just talk, and you know it. I'm not even sure of what a real pyromaniac is."

"Neither am I. Let's discuss it for a moment. Perhaps we can find out something."

"Yes," I said. But I didn't want to discuss it, didn't want to find out—something.

I let him do the talking.

"First of all, let's think about fire. Fire is elemental, you know. The spark of life. The fire of the sun; heat, light, motion. We all recognize it, and it attracts us. That's why the color red is so important; the most primitive, the most exciting color—the first color perceived by an infant. Red is fire."

"It's also blood," I said.

"Correct. And blood is life, too, in the symbol-language we all use. So fire is blood and fire is life, and fire is something else as well. It's magic.

"You'll find the fire-magic in all the legends of all the cultures we know. The Parsees worship fire as prescribed by Zoroaster. Vesta and Agni were fire-deities. You've heard the old story of Prometheus, who stole the gift of fire from the gods—it's common in other religions as well as the Greek. Our own Bible is full of associations between fire and the supernatural. The story of Moses and the burning bush; the pillar of fire that guided the Israelites."

"Haloes," I added. "And the angels with the flaming swords."

"Right. And fire has always been used when dealing with the supernatural. Consider the altar fires, the fire kindled for sacrifice, the ritual of burning the heretic or the witch at the stake. And let's not forget the dominant concept of the fires of Hell. Even the medieval alchemists thought they could find the philosopher's stone in mercurial fire and water. Fire has always been mysterious—a source of life and creation, and a source of death and destruction. It's magic. Even a child recognizes that. When you set a fire you're creating a new world, and at the same time you're destroying an old one. Fire-setting is a simple act. I'd say that our statistics show seventy percent of all pyromaniacs have an intelligence below the accepted norm."

"Then you do know something about pyromania?"

"A little." He went over to the bookshelves, rummaged around, and returned with a volume which he opened and examined. "The American Psychiatric Association classification listing comes under Psychasthenia and Complusive States (002-X21) with symptomatic manifestations, pyromania (902). Does that tell you anything?"

"No." I hesitated. "Except, from what you've told me, most firebugs are imbeciles or morons who have a compulsion to set fires. But why? And what about the thirty percent who have normal intelligence or above? Why would they start fires?"

"That's the question, isn't it?"

"Don't look at me," I said. "I haven't any ideas."

"Are you certain?" Schwarm opened his notebook. "What does the word 'fire' mean to you? What other words does it suggest? Let's see what you can associate with 'fire' now."

"Well—words and phrases, of course. Ball of fire. Fire-water. Hellfire. Creative fire. Spark of genius. You're fired. Playing with fire. Hot seat. You burn me up. Fight fire with fire. Better to marry than to burn. Hot number. Carrying the torch. Seeing red. Fires of love. Old flame. Hot mama. Heat of passion." I shrugged. "That enough?"

"Plenty. Now, let's examine what you've just told me. What do these phrases suggest to you?"

"Some of them refer to punishment, don't they? Hell and the hot sea. Getting angry. And most of them have a sexual meaning."

"Exactly. We all use these figures of speech in our daily vocabulary. But some people actually think in these terms, and for them the phrases have a very real connotation.

"It's not surprising to find that most firebugs begin their careers in their late adolescence. That's the period when sexual maladjustment may precipitate paranoid schizophrenia. Jealousy, rivalry, impotence or frigidity, perversion and fetichism may all play a part. Setting a fire seems to release a tension in such cases.

"Symbolically, you see, fire-setting is the sex-act. It may be the substitute for incest or some other forbidden form of sexual experience. It is something feared yet desired. Some fire-setters feel they can control fires better than their own emotions. Others feel that fire is a more potent instrument than themselves. In either case, the release from tension is there—temporarily. But since it does not solve the basic situation, the act must be repeated. That's what makes your firebug."

"But if a person knows this, wouldn't he seek help?" I asked.

"That's just the point. Most pyromaniacs refuse to admit the truth, even to themselves. Some of them operate in an amnesic trance. Others hear voices that command them. They have the feeling that the fire was started by someone other than themselves. And they aren't concerned about the harm they do—they worry more over what the authorities think of them. Symbolically to destroy love, or loved ones, isn't wrong to them. Because all fire-setters are potential murderers, capable of acting on impulse when thwarted. I had one youngster in here with all of the classical symptoms: enuresis, cyclothymic traits. And the urethral sadism component. He used to bite the heads of his pet white mice."

"Charming," I said. "The part about the mice I understand. The rest sounds too complicated for me. Can't you put it into English, Doc?"

"Of course. Think of it this way. Most pyromaniacs come from a poor environment. There's a bad family situation—broken home, sexual promiscuity on the part of one or both parents. Your typical pyromaniac—although I hesitate to describe any case as 'typical'—is a compliant son who adores his mother but hates his stepfather or any man she associates with, and suspects her of moral transgressions.

"He is afraid to rebel openly, however, so he runs away. Runs into alcohol, into an unfortunate early marriage. Often the situation is complicated by an unfortunate physical defect or blemish which makes a feeling of being rejected or unwanted doubly disturbing. Outwardly, of course, your firebug is a conformist.

"He never quarrels openly with authority. He appears to be gregarious, cooperative; but when a situation becomes intolerable, he runs away. Runs away from mother, runs away from home, from the job, from the armed forces, from any adjustment with reality which seems unpleasant. And it's not his fault, he reasons. It's his father who punished him, who gave him his physical defect, who mistreated and deserted his mother, who violated her. He hates his father, but dares not openly defy him even in his own mind. So he runs away, runs away into fantasy where an evil voice—father, of course, in disguise—tells him to set the fire. Or gives him the feelings which he cannot openly satisfy, and for which he substitutes by arson."

"You head-shrinkers are always bringing sex into it," I said.

Schwarm shook his head. "We don't *bring*

anything. We merely try to find what is already there. And in pyromania the sexual parallel seems obvious. Tension—the urge for gratification becoming irresistible—then exaltation and release."

"Interesting," I said. "But where do I fit in? You gave me some tests, Doc. What's the verdict?"

Schwarm lighted another cigarette. "Supposing you tell me what you think."

I hesitated a moment. "I don't seem to fit the pattern very well, do I? My parent were happy together, and there was nothing disturbing in my childhood. I'm not an adolescent any more, I have no physical handicap, I'm not too much of an outward conformist or inward rebel. And I don't get any of my kicks from lighting fires or turning in alarms; as I told you, fire frightens me. But what did the tests indicate?"

"Just what you told me. You're not a pyromaniac, though there's always a potential threat." He bent his head, then looked. "But there's a great preoccupation with fire. Almost a pyrophobia. And you've said a half-dozen times that fire frightens you. Why?"

"I don't know."

"Is there some incident, earlier, involving fire—?"

"I don't know."

"What about your dreams, Phil? Ever have any dreams about—?"

There was the sound of a door opening in the outer office. The Marines had landed. "You've got company, Doc," I said, standing up. "Maybe we can kick this around some more at another time."

"Good." He rose. "Phil, I think I could help you, if only you'd let me. And you could help yourself."

"Sure." I started for the door.

"Want to take the other way out?" He indicated a second door at the left. "I'm expecting some other people this morning. Dalton asked me to give them the same checkup."

"Good enough. Thanks for your time and trouble."

"You'll be home if—if anyone needs to get in touch with you?"

"I'm not planning to skip town, Doc," I told him. "So just tell your friend Dalton he needn't worry. I'm going to stick around for the—" I had my hand on the doorknob, and I felt like going out before saying that last word.

Schwarm said it for me. "Fireworks?"

"That's right." I grinned. "Pyromaniacs of the world—ignite!"

9

I GOT HOME about nine and slept until half past three. A couple of times the dream started, but I always managed to wake up before it really got going. Then I'd doze off again. When I got up I felt better.

I was just finishing my shower when the phone rang. I dripped my way over to it.

"Hello?"

"Phil? Ed Cronin. Where the hell you been?"

"Read the papers."

"*You* read the papers! What's happening in this city, anyway? Send you out to get a couple of simple little feature yarns and you land right in the middle of the biggest local story we've hit in three years."

"*Phil Dempster, Star Reporter,*" I said. "Did

you call me up to tell me you want my autograph?"

"I want your copy," Cronin yelled. "Right now!"

"But the yarn's dead," I told him. "The fire killed it. Everytime I go out and try to make an honest buck, somebody burns my bridges ahead of me."

"What do you mean, the yarn's dead? It's hotter than ever. You found Ricardi's body, didn't you? There's what we want. Never mind the cults. A *Globe* reporter, working on a special assignment, stumbles across—oh, you heard me. Read the paper!"

"You got a write-up?"

"Of course we have. Swiped your photo off the dust jacket of the book. Gave it a big play. Now we want a follow-up for tomorrow. Exclusive statement. How soon can you get me a thousand words? I want to put it on AP—"

"Look, Cronin, I've got to get busy and do one of those articles for you. If I can find a cult that doesn't burn up before I get to it."

"Never mind that stuff now. This is important."

"Twelve hundred bucks is more important to me."

"So we'll pay you the dough, articles or no articles. When do I get my thousand words?"

I looked at my watch. "You there until six?"

"Sure."

"I'll be down."

"Comb your hair. We'll take another picture."

"Anything you say. Want me to pose in a fire-helmet?"

"Shut up and go to work."

I shut up and went to work. I did him a thousand words on the Church of the Golden Atom. I worked in my little clown-face friend, and played him up as the key figure in the mystery. It wasn't hard to do, because I was telling the truth. *He* knew what was going on, and why. And I was just a stooge.

But why?

I couldn't answer that one, and I didn't try. I finished the yarn up, hopped in the car, and took it downtown. Cronin was waiting for me under the big clock in his office.

I threw the pages on his desk and pointed. "Fifteen minutes early," I said. "How's that for speed?"

He grunted and tossed me a paper. "You read this while I read your stuff."

I did. It was quite a story. The way Cronin angled it, I—or the *Globe*, rather—was a hero. And I—meaning the *Globe* again—was going to solve the mysterious fire-deaths that were spreading terror throughout the city.

"Terror throughout the city." Big deal. But he wrote it like that, played it up big. Half of the front page was devoted to the fire. I saw my picture, Dalton's picture, Ricardi's picture. There was a big story on Ricardi, using much of the material I had in the notebook—apparently the reporter who dug up the original dope was working on the assignment.

I noted that an inquest would be held Saturday—tomorrow morning. And the police were looking for my little friend. Good. That meant Dalton had taken my report seriously after all.

In fact, everybody was taking this seriously. Perhaps Cronin hadn't exaggerated the terror angle. One of his snoops had been out rounding up comments from housewives who were buying locks at hardware stores, family men who were purchasing shotgun shells. The police were rounding up suspects, checking on every known or suspected arsonist in town. The heat—and I winced as I thought of it—was on.

"Good enough!" Cronin thwacked down the pages. "I'll just jazz this up a little and run it tomorrow. Come on upstairs now and get yourself mugged."

"You're really serious?"

"Damned right." We climbed the steps in the hall. "From now on, you stick to this yarn. Maybe you can pick up some leads tomorrow at the inquest. Maybe some of our boys will find something out. Whatever they get I'll pass along to you. The old man wants to play this story for all it's worth. And you're the logical byline for anything that breaks."

"Including my neck."

"You getting scared?"

"Not me. I already *got* scared last night. I wasn't fooling about this little loony, you know. He stuck a knife in my ribs."

"Think he set the fire?"

"Not this last one. He couldn't have. But he

might have set the first. And he knows all about it. There's something going on, something connected with these cults."

"Your job is to find out about it."

"My job," I said, "is to stay alive."

Cronin stood silent as the photographer pushed me into a chair, seared me with his spots, and took three shots in rapid succession.

"That's it," he told me. I got up. Cronin put his arm around my shoulder.

"You can't let me down, Phil. Not when you're in this deep."

"Any deeper and I'll be in a grave."

"Nonsense. I'm not asking you to take any chances. Just keep your eyes open. If we can feed you a lead, follow it up. Routine stuff, really. But there may be a chance to hit the jackpot."

"I'll bet that will make Captain Dalton ever so happy," I said. "To know that one of his principal suspects has turned detective."

"Flush Captain Dalton," Cronin advised. "He's got nothing on you, Phil. Believe me, I made it my business to find out. Look, he's going to call you for the inquest tomorrow anyway. You'll have to be there. So why not earn yourself some quick money by sticking on the assignment? If nothing turns up, do us a Sunday story on this little guy. Go interview some doctors, find out about the pyromaniac bit."

I grinned. "That I've done already," I said.

"All right. Contact me right after the inquest

tomorrow morning. I'll have two reps there anyway, but I want your slant."

"Will do."

I left him in the corridor and took the elevator down. It was time to eat.

The Dinner Gong was crowded, but I found a booth where I could eat alone. Only I wasn't alone. A copperhaired girl sat across from me, and next to her was a white-faced man with bleeding lips. Next to him was the golden countenance of Professor Ricardi, but it wasn't golden any more—it was purple, mottled and inflamed. And as I stared at it, the face began to change, to melt into another charred and mutilated mask. I jerked my eyes away and now they rested on another occupant. Doctor Schwarm, I believe. Doctor Schwarm, who knew that anyone who has a morbid fear of fire may be a potential pyromaniac, who knew that sometimes a firebug doesn't remember what he's done. Alcohol sets him off, and then he wanders out in a daze, and when the flames rise he isn't sure of what happened. And if he dreams of fire, and there was an earlier time he won't talk about, then maybe—

I blinked until the thoughts went away, the faces vanished. Silly business. You couldn't get four people into the booth-seat across from me. Absolutely impossible. A lunatic, a neurotic girl, a dead cult-leader and a head-shrinker. What a combination! Why did I let it bother me? I was alone. *All alone.*

That thought didn't exactly cheer me up,

either. I was all alone, but somewhere out there in the city was another. A man I'd never met, but who knew about me. He must know now, because he'd read the papers. He'd know I was dangerous to his plans, and he was clever enough to act.

Schwarm was probably right when he said that most firebugs were adolescent and sub-normal. But these two crimes weren't the work of an adolescent. They weren't the work of a sub-normal individual, either. Abnormal would be the proper term. Abnormal, and abnormally cunning. These fires had been set for a purpose. It wasn't arson, but murder.

Schwarm had told me that, too. "All firebugs are potential murderers."

And *this* one wasn't a potential but an *actual* killer. This man, who knew about me. Who might come after me, knowing I was all alone.

I couldn't finish my meal. I had to get out of there. When I started the car, I had to fight to keep it headed for home. Now was the time to run for it, to run away, far away.

Isn't that what Schwarm had said? Firebugs are weak, they run away from reality.

Well?

Was I or wasn't I?

The only way to find out would be to stick around. And I wanted to know. A part of me *had* to know. So I'd stick. But I'd be careful. I'd watch myself, make sure that Dalton and the cops knew my whereabouts. No more foolish chances, no more late evening prowls.

It was still twilight, and that helped. The street-lights came on with reassuring brilliance. Rows of mechanical candles to guide my way home. *Fire is dangerous, but it gives light, and light protects us from darkness. The Powers of Darkness. We fear fire but we fear the dark more. Why? Red is light, black is death.*

I turned the corner and parked, crossed the street. Then I saw it, looming before me in front of the entrance. It was a big car, and it was black. Jet black. Black as death.

Somebody was waiting for me.

Only a few hours had passed, and already, somebody was waiting. Waiting in a big black hearse.

I halted, hesitated. I tried to see into the car out of the corner of my eye, but couldn't. And I really didn't want to. Curiosity wasn't going to kill this cat. Sweat oozed across my forehead and I was suddenly acutely conscious that I knew more than anybody else did about the cults, that I had been the first man on the scene in two murders. Perhaps I had seen something I shouldn't have and had been too drunk the first time to realize what it was and too scared the second. But somebody else might now know that. Somebody else might assume I knew far more than I did, that my supposed knowledge and Captain Dalton's authority might be the perfect match ... match.

There was still time to turn around, walk back to my own car, get in, drive away. Chances are, I'd be followed. But at least I could get onto the main drag, head for the stationhouse. Dalton would protect me. It was worth a try.

I turned, took two steps.

Then the car-door swung open, on the street side. And the voice reached me.

"Mr. Dempster! I want to see you."

The voice was low and musical. A woman's voice. I glanced over and saw the streetlight haloing blonde hair. "Please, Mr. Dempster. I must talk to you at once. I'm Agatha Loodens."

I turned and crossed the street again to meet Ricardi's mistress.

10

AGATHA LOODENS leaned back on my sofa, holding a glass in her hand. It matched her outfit
perfectly; the maize dress, the gold button
earrings, the straight blonde hair gathered in a
bun at the nape of her bare neck. Looking at
the glass and then at her, I realized she had
highball-colored hair.

"Comfortable?" I asked.

"Very." She smiled. Her teeth were very
white and very regular. Everything was *very*
about her.

"Then suppose you tell me what it is you
wanted to see me about."

She laughed. Very musical laugh. "You're
quite direct, Mr. Dempster. I had hope we might
consider this in the nature of a social call."

"You mean a wake?" I said. "After all, Joe's dead—"

"Please." She wasn't laughing now. "I'd rather we didn't talk about that."

"I kind of thought that was what you came here to talk about."

"Not exactly." She leaned forward, setting her glass down on the coffee-table which separated my chair from the sofa.

"But—you called him Joe. How did you know his real name?"

"It's in the papers," I answered. "All of it."

She nodded. "Of course." Then she picked up her glass again. Before she drank she said, "Or almost all of it."

"Meaning?"

"I was hoping you'd tell me."

I stood up and walked over to the dinette table where I mixed myself another drink. "This isn't a training-camp," I said. "Do your sparring someplace else."

"That's rude."

"I'm a rude man. A rude man, and a tired one. I've been through a lot these past three days. I've had all the cross-examinations anybody could possibly need. Police, reporters, a psychiatrist—"

"Oh! Then you saw Dr. Schwarm too. Did he make you take that quaint little test of his?"

I nodded. "I took the quaint little test. In case you're interested, I passed with flying colors, too." I walked back, sat down, leaned forward. "Which means, Mrs. Loodens, that

I'm not a firebug, if that's what you want to know."

"Why, I never even considered the possibility. You have a very suspicious mind, Mr. Dempster."

"Right. And while we're still on the subject, what about you? How did you score on the ink-blots?"

She took another sir, a very delicate sip. "I didn't see any lamps or torches or burning brands, if that's what you mean. I'm afraid my reactions were purely—feminine. In fact, I think I may have shocked the doctor just a trifle." She smiled and stretched back. Her skirt crept a bit higher on her leg. At another time I might have been interested. Chronologically, she could be a year or two older than I, but exceptionally well-preserved. Maybe she took ATOMIC ENERGY CAPSULES and used VITAL CREAM. Come to think of it, I was sure she did.

I forced myself back to the business at hand. "Now that we've had our medical report, what is it you wanted to ask me? Is it a deal you're after?"

"Perhaps." She leaned forward. "Did you ever meet Amos Peabody?"

"No."

"You know nothing about his outfit?"

"His religious organization?"

"I said 'outfit,' Mr. Dempster. Let's be frank— he was running a racket, the same as Joe."

"You admit it?"

"Why not?" Agatha Loodens adjusted an

earring. "I wouldn't insult your intelligence by pretending otherwise. The Church of the Golden Atom was a nice little grift. In time, it might have become a nice big grift. But it's too late now, because of what happened. And that's why it interests me. What happened—and why."

I stared at her. "Suppose you ask your attorney, Mr. Weatherbee."

Her eyes narrowed. "What made you say that?"

"Seems natural he'd have a theory. After all, isn't he a partner?"

"He was, until last month." She sipped her drink. "Or do you already know that?"

"News to me."

"There was a dispute last month, about future plans. Mr. Weatherbee had some idea about combining with other outfits, with Joe as the leader. Joe couldn't see it. So Don pulled out and we went on alone."

I took her glass for a refill and talked over my shoulder. "Very interesting," I said. "Here you are, the three of you, coining money in a going, growing cult racket. And just because Weatherbee's plan is rejected, he pulls out. Gives up a nice, soft, steady source of income he's worked to build up for years. How idealistic!"

She almost yanked the glass out of my hand when I offered it to her. "Are you being sarcastic?"

"Very," I told her. "As the British are so fond

of saying, I put it to you. I put it to you that your friend Joe—Professor Ricardi to his devoted followers—kicked Weatherbee out. I put it you that he discovered Weatherbee had other ideas."

"What kind of ideas would those be?"

"The same ideas any man might get if he spent too much time around you."

"Really!" She laughed. "I've never been so complimentarily insulted in all my—"

"Never mind that. Is it true?"

Agatha Loodens sighed. "Yes. Don started to get ideas. And Joe threatened to beat him up."

I nodded. "And that was enough to scare Weatherbee away from a sure twenty or thirty thousand dollars a year? Please, Mrs. Loodens. I'm going to have to put it to you again. I think Joe had the goods on Weatherbee—something he wanted to keep hushed up—and threatened to spill it unless he got out."

She didn't answer. And that was answer enough for me. "Just what was this secret Weatherbee guarded so closely?"

"I don't know."

"Ricardi never told you, eh?" I moved closer to her, and Agatha Loodens stared at me. She had little gold flecks in the pupils of her eyes.

"I put it to you that Weatherbee's guilty secret concerned your late husband—perhaps the way he died."

She raised one hand to her mouth, and I knew I'd hit the jackpot.

"Weatherbee had something to do with your

husband's death. You and Ricardi knew it. But you didn't care, because you were all profiting by it together. Until Weatherbee got ambitious and tried to move in on you. Ricardi threatened him and made him leave the setup."

I nodded to myself. "Now it makes sense. You came to me because you're wondering if Weatherbee could be behind these fires. You're wondering if he bumped off your boy-friend."

"Yes, it's true. That's the reason."

"*Did* Weatherbee murder your husband?"

"I don't know. I swear it, I don't know. Joe knew, but he wouldn't tell me. He didn't want me to get mixed up in it."

"And you never went to the police. You never wanted to because it might spoil your setup. I see."

"No you don't. The way you tell it, I sound like a criminal—suspecting a man of being involved in my husband's death, and not doing anything about it. But it wasn't that simple. Nothing's ever that simple. I loved Joe, and if I went to the police, what would they think about that? You know the answer. They'd try and make it appear as though I helped plan the killing. Weatherbee would see to that. He'll do anything to get what he wants, anything."

"He wanted you," I said. "So you think he arranged to murder Joe last night."

She nodded. "That why I wanted to see you. To find out if there was anything more you might know about this. To see if Weatherbee had gotten to you, in case you did know, and threatened you so you'd keep silent."

"Supposing he had," I answered. "What did you plan on doing then?"

Agatha Loodens stood up. "I had my choice of two methods of persuasion," she told me. "The first was—this."

She opened her purse. Her hand dipped in delicately and emerged with a small revolver.

"Interesting method," I said. "And what about the other alternative? Would that be interesting, too?"

"You'd be the judge," she murmured. She took three steps forward around the coffee-table, then leaned over me. I didn't have to raise my arms to pull her down. She melted into my lap, tossing her purse to the floor. Melted like molten lava. The heat poured from her body, fusing her mouth to mine.

I was to be the judge, eh? Well, court was now in session. I stared down into those gold-flecked, eyes, then stared past them to the floor.

The purse rested there where she'd dropped it—and from its open throat protruded a score of little tongues. Some red, some black, some white, some green.

I pushed her off my lap. "Excuse me," I said. "You dropped something." I stooped and picked up one of the tongues. "Book-matches, I believe." I picked up a handful and then another. "Didn't know you smoked."

"I don't smoke. I—I collect book-matches.

It's a hobby. You've heard of that, haven't you?"

"I've heard of lots of hobbies."

She clung to my arm. "Please, it's the truth! You don't think I had anything to do with—"

The phone rang.

I straightened up. She was on her feet instantly. "Don't answer it!" she whispered, as if the phone itself could hear her.

I pushed her away. She watched me cross the room, pick up the telephone. She heard my voice, heard it with her ears, her eyes, her mouth, her very body intent and intense.

She watched as I put the phone down, walked back. And then her arms were around me again. "Who was it? Was is Weatherbee?"

"It was Captain Dalton."

"Anything—?"

"No. Just checking."

Her frightened breathing was replaced by a slower, more languorous inhalation. Her fingers began to trace a pattern on my shoulders. Her head came up. I stared straight into her golden eyes.

"Captain Dalton had a message for me," I murmured. "He told me to be a good little boy and go straight to bed. Because tomorrow morning I must be up bright and early. To attend your lover's inquest."

She jerked away, scooped up her purse.

"I'm glad to see you're taking his advice, too," I said. "And here's something else to remember."

133

Agatha Loodens opened the door so fast I didn't think she'd hear my parting words. But she did, because the door slammed shut behind her the moment I'd uttered them.

"Little girls like you," I said, "shouldn't play with matches."

11

IT WASN'T until the next morning that I realized
what a fool I'd been. Me and my big mouth. I
should have kept that big mouth silent, left it
where it belonged. It was having a pretty good
time, as I remembered.

And if I'd gone on, perhaps I would have
found out a lot of things. Some of them might
have been very pleasant, and some of them
might have been very unpleasant.

As is was, I knew nothing. Could Agatha
Loodens have started those fires? Did she set
the first one as a blind, to make it appear that
somebody was out to destroy cults and cult-
leaders—so as to mislead suspicion when she
killed Ricardi?

With Weatherbee out of the picture, and

Ricardi dead, she was left in control of the Church of the Golden Atom. Not a razed structure, but perfectly intact. A· nice setup.

But would she kill her lover?

Perhaps. She certainly hadn't behaved like one bereft last night.

Then again, with Ricardi gone, who'd front for the cult as leader?

She might plan on taking over that role herself, come to think of it. Or she could have another candidate, already chosen, in the background.

That was a possibility. Figure it as cold-blooded arson, completely and ruthlessly motivated.

I thought about it while I shaved and fixed breakfast and made myself pretty for the inquest. I thought about a lot of things.

There was another angle to consider, too, where Mrs. Loodens was concerned. Those book-matches. Suppose she didn't have any particular plan, but merely a compulsion. A compulsion to start fires.

Whoever killed Ricardi had chosen a hideous method. If Agatha Loodens hated her lover, she'd certainly indicated it in the manner she used to destroy him. I wondered what kind of background and fantasies she had. What makes female firebugs burn?

Then again, according to her story, she feared this attorney, Don Weatherbee. Feared him, and suspected him of causing her husband's death. Maybe she'd told me the truth, or part of the truth. I reviewed my gallery of suspects, now. Agatha Loodens, Weatherbee, the clown-faced man or his associates in the White Brotherhood, plus that old familiar figure of song and story—person or persons unknown.

Unless Captain Dalton and his boys had been working overtime, I rather anticipated the inquest would pin the rap on the latter suspect.

And of course, I was right.

They'd arranged a rather unusual setting for the affair. Dalton sent one of his blue-uniformed chauffeurs to call for me, and I was surprised when we drew up in front of 1902 Benson Street. They were holding the inquest in Ricardi's home! The place smelled of smoke, but downstairs was intact.

Afterwards, I realized why. A man named Kleber had swung the deal—an investigator for the National Board of Fire Underwriters. Ricardi's place was covered by insurance. He seemed to have gone over the place thoroughly some time yesterday. When I came in, Dalton immediately took my arm and steered me over to Kleber. The tall, grey-haired investigator was pleasantly persistent. He asked me for a full account of the whole affair, and I told him what I knew. He'd gotten it all from Dalton, of course, but he wanted it again.

Later on he got it still a third time, when they put me up for testimony.

Quite an audience had assembled to listen to me. The fire marshal, several of his men,

Dalton, a detective named Henderson, Ricardi's part-time housekeeper, and several more familiar faces.

The police and the jury sat on one side of the room. As I was examined by Finch, the coroner, I could see my friends sitting on the other side. There was Schwarm, of course, next to Doctor Oakes—he lived down the block, and he'd come over after I dragged Ricardi out and pronounced him dead. Next to Schwarm on the left was a short, squat, balding man in grey tweeds. I guessed he might be Don Weatherbee, and I guessed right—realized that when I caught him glaring at Agatha Loodens.

She was there, too, and glared right back. First at Weatherbee, and then at me.

Just one big happy family, if only the clown-faced man were here.

I wished for his presence very much, particularly when they called me and Finch asked his questions. The more I mentioned him in my story, the more worried I got—especially when I glanced over at the jury to see how they were taking it. No apparent reaction at all on those six stony faces.

For the first time I realized this occasion could be serious—these six dead-pan citizens had it within their power to indict me.

I told Finch all I knew. Schwarm smiled up at me, but all the other faces were cold, on both sides of the room. Captain Dalton and Kleber were whispering from time to time with another well-dressed man whom I vaguely recognized as the District Attorney. I didn't like that, either.

When I'd finished, I paid particular attention to the rest of the proceedings. They called Oakes, and he and the Coroner traded medical Latin for a few minutes, both gravely arriving at the conclusion that Joseph Clutt, *alias* Professor Ricardi, was legally dead and had legally died in an illegal conflagration.

The part-time housekeeper contributed her bit. She hadn't been in to clean for three days beforehand. There were questions about the disposition of rags and bedding, but nothing important.

Before I was called, several Golden Atom witnesses had established the fact that Ricardi had left the Church following the meeting the other night and driven off in his own car, alone. He had stated his intention of going straight home to bed—he thought he was catching cold. Apparently ATOMIC ENERGY CAPSULES did not contain antihistamine. But none of them had overheard or noticed anything suspicious. Ricardi got no messages, no phone-calls; he wasn't agitated or upset.

So the story gradually took shape—with everything apparent but a coherent plot. Ricardi went home, I discovered his body, he was pronounced dead.

Now came the rest of the witnesses. Weatherbee, first. He had a deep, courtroom voice, out of Blackstone by Old Taylor, and a wonderfully professional way of using that voice to say absolutely nothing.

Yes, he had previously been affiliated with Professor Ricardi in a professional capacity. Their arrangement had terminated several months ago—he named the date. No disagreement; it was merely that the pressure of legal work prevented him from further fulfilling his obligations to the corporate Church. He absolutely denied having seen Professor Ricardi on the night of his death or at any time since the severance of their business relationship.

On the night of the fire he had been playing poker at the home of a friend. Captain Dalton's testimony would corroborate this.

The Coroner violated procedure and asked Dalton for confirmation. He got it.

Then Mrs. Loodens came on. She gave a good performance. This morning she appeared in black—trimmed with tears. It was all so dreadful, so very dreadful. She didn't know a thing about it. And to think she hadn't even been there at the Church on that last evening! She'd been home, with a *very* bad headache. And of course, she had witnesses. The maid, and then some friends who spoke to her over the telephone at about the time of the fire. Captain Dalton knew.

It appeared, when the Coroner turned to him again, that Captain Dalton did know.

Exit, Mrs. Loodens. I caught Weatherbee glaring at her as she took her seat again, and he noticed me. It may have been a trick of the light, but I thought for an instant that he winked.

Now Kleber was on the stand. Expert testimony, this. The fire was definitely not accidental. Whoever seized and bound Ricardi had also deliberately kindled the blaze. Whoever knocked him over the head—

I blinked. How had that escaped me? But come to think of it, that was the only possible way to account for Ricardi's being tied. Somebody had knocked him out, first.

I followed Kleber's story closely now, cutting through the technicalities and listening to some of the questions he posed.

First of all, how did the murderer get in the house? All the doors and windows were locked when the firemen and police arrived—all except the French window which I claimed to have broken in my entrance. The jurors had toured the house.

If my testimony was valid—and I didn't relish the way he came down on the *if*—it meant one thing. Ricardi must have admitted his murderer himself, done so willingly. What followed is conjectural in the extreme. Was Ricardi slugged downstairs and his body carried up to the bedroom? Or did the assault occur there? No evidence one way or the other. But it might have a bearing on the matter.

More important, for the purposes of this hearing, was the indication of *haste*. Obviously the crime had been committed in a great hurry. In his opinion, the object was definitely not murder. The blow on the skull hadn't killed Ricardi. Anyone whose primary purpose was the death of Ricardi would have continued to batter in his head until he was dead.

No, the real motive was arson. The fire had been quickly improvised and deliberately so, beyond the shadow of a doubt. The house was fully covered by insurance—and the beneficiary was the corporation. Kleber would leave it to the jury regarding the matter of murder and possible suspects. But he wanted to emphasize that this was a clear-cut case of arson.

I saw what he was getting at, now. Arson meant intent to defraud—no insurance claim would be paid. Very neat. And I wasn't the only one who saw it, either. Agatha Looden's eyes were wide. *She* was the corporation, of course, and we all knew it.

Then Schwarm took the stand. More expert testimony. I listened, wondering whether he'd say something to pin the rap on Mrs. Loodens. Or on me.

He did a beautiful job. First, the medical definition of pyromania. Then, a report of his examinations of Mrs. Loodens, Weatherbee, and myself. Plus—this was a surprise—the part-time housekeeper.

His considered opinion, as a qualified psychiatrist, was that none of us were pyromaniacal.

Kleber grinned. Clear case of arson, now. Or so he thought.

So he thought until Schwarm went on, speaking quietly and deliberately. He went over the same evidence Kleber had offered and turned it inside out.

He cited the usual motives for arson, then demolished them, one by one. If Weatherbee killed Ricardi for revenge, he certainly wouldn't have bungled the firesetting. In order to conceal the crime effectively, he had only to make use of materials at hand. There was plenty of oil in the basement, for example; he could have kindled a blaze that would spread swiftly and surely. Besides, there was his alibi.

As for Mrs. Loodens, her motive might have been to collect on the insurance. But she was wealthy in her own right, and the twenty-thousand-dollar payment to the corporation wouldn't materially increase her holdings. And even if she acted out of jealousy or anger, she most certainly would have set a fire that was sure to blaze up. Also, she had an alibi, too.

In the matter of Philip Dempster—that was me, now—there was certainly no apparent suspicion of any motive. I didn't know Ricardi. I had nothing to profit from by his death. And the best substantiation for my statement was the fact that somebody had turned in an alarm. Since no one had showed up to admit it, the logical assumption was that my own statement was correct—the mysterious cultist had called the firemen and fled. Surely I wouldn't assault Ricardi, start a crude fire, then run out and summon the engines, run back inside, and bring Ricardi down. And Schwarm had been with me earlier in the evening, he knew I hadn't time to undertake such a mission. So I had an alibi, too.

No, this wasn't the work of an arsonist. This was a case of pyromania, in his opinion.

Everything Kleber had said pointed to it. The element of *haste* showed that the criminal had absolutely no premeditation. The fire itself was *improvised*, apparently on the spur of the moment. Nothing was planned—in all probability, the whole series of activities were spontaneous. It was Doctor Schwarm's view that the murderer was definitely a pyromaniac, and still at large.

That did it.

There was more testimony and discussion, of course, and Coroner Finch got in his nickel's worth. But the verdict was as fast as it was foregone.

Professor Ricardi had met death at the hands of a person or persons unknown.

Exit smiling. No applause, but some of us felt like it. Not Captain Dalton, of course, and not Mr. Kleber.

I nodded to the *Globe* reporters Cronin had sent down, and gave one of them a message for him—I'd have his story over this afternoon some time.

Then I jostled through the crowd looking for Schwarm. He was talking to Mrs. Loodens. As I approached, an arm reached out and clung.

"Mr. Dempster."

I turned. Weatherbee was at my side. "I wonder if I might have a word with you."

"Why—yes, I guess so."

"Let's get out of here, then. My car's right outside."

I allowed myself to be dragged away. Weatherbee and I went out together and climbed into his shiny new Lincoln. Very appropriate car for an attorney, come to think of it. Lincoln was a lawyer, too—but if he were alive today, I doubt if he'd have the kind of practice which would allow him to buy an automobile like this. It was heavy and slick. Like Weatherbee himself.

"Where to now?" I said.

"Thought we might have lunch together."

"I'm sorry. I've got to get a story out. Couldn't you drive me back to my place and talk on the way?"

"If you like." He gunned out into the street. "So you're covering this case for the *Globe*, eh? What do you think of the deal?"

"I think Schwarm's right. It's the work of a firebug."

"Does Mrs. Loodens think so too?"

"How would I know?"

"Didn't she tell you? She was up to your place last night."

I didn't answer. He grinned to himself. "Mind if I asked what she wanted?"

"I don't mind. She wanted the same thing you do—information."

"What'd she say about me?"

"She merely told about breaking up the partnership."

He chuckled again. "I'll bet she did." The car picked up speed and so did my heart. It occurred to me belatedly that Weatherbee was as much a suspect as anybody else. And I had delivered myself into his hands like a Christmas basket to a needy family. Once out in the forest preserves and I could be tomorrow morning's headlines. How did you jump out of a speeding car? Jam the door open and double up so you'd roll like a ball when you hit? Crank open the windows and holler for a cop? Or sit there, as I was doing, and drown in my sweat. Better to drown than to burn . . .

"She think I killed Ricardi?"

I didn't answer.

"Good enough for me. But I didn't, boy. He had it coming to him, of course—only murder's not my business."

"What is your business, Mr. Weatherbee?" I asked. "Is it spying on Mrs. Loodens and me?"

No chuckle now. "That's kind of a harsh remark, Mr. Dempster. A fellow could resent a remark like that."

"I resent being cross-examined, too."

He sighed. "Minute ago you made a crack about what my business might be. I'll tell you, and you can make up your own mind if you want to keep it confidential or not. I'm in the cult business, Mr. Dempster."

"But I thought you and Ricardi split up?"

"That we did."

"Then—?"

"Ricardi wasn't the only one running a cult

in this town. There's the Wisdom outfit, and the New Kingdom gang, and the House of Truth, the White Brotherhood. Nobody knows it, but I happen to be the attorney for Dykes, of the House of Truth. And last month, after the split with Ricardi, I paid a little visit to Amos Peabody. He was quite a sharpie, that boy. I told him how I'd dragged Ricardi out of the gutter by the scruff of his neck and built the Golden Atom deal up. I told him I could do the same thing for the White Brotherhood. Take it out of the penny-ante evangelist class and really streamline his operation, put him in the big leagues. Make a long story short, I bought in on him. I owned fifty percent of the White Brotherhood Tabernacle. And somebody killed Peabody, burned the place down.

"Now do you see why I'm interested?"

I nodded. "I'm beginning to."

"Maybe you can see something else, Dempster. Two fires have been started. Two cult heads have died in them. What does that suggest?"

"Somebody wants to knock off cult leaders."

"Very brilliant observation. Maybe you can also figure out the reason why."

"Rivalry?" I suggested.

We pulled up in front of my apartment. "Go to the head of the class." His eyes narrowed. "Better still, go to the meeting tonight and see Ogundu."

"Ogundu?"

"Don't know him, eh? He's a cult-leader, too. Runs the Temple of the Living Flame on the south side. Does that suggest anything to you?"

"Firebug?"

"Firebugs, in the plural. Every torch in town must hang around his setup, getting their kicks."

"Why don't you tell Captain Dalton what you think?"

"Don't be dumb. I tell Dalton, he asks me why I'm interested. I tell him that, he tells the paper. I get my name out in the open. Not good."

"But I'm working for the paper myself."

"I know that. And you're a smart operator. You'll be able to get in where the cops can't."

"It's a good lead," I said. "I'll look into it. But if I do get a story, I don't see how I can keep your name out of it."

"Well, you've got plenty of time to figure a way," Weatherbee told me. "I don't want to be tied to any cult deal. All I want is a line on Ogundu and his Temple."

"Read the papers," I said. "I'll get a story of some kind if I go there tonight. Probably run it Monday."

"Maybe. If I say so."

"What do you mean?"

"You're not doing this for the papers, Dempster. You're doing this for me. I want to get a report from you tomorrow, in person. If it's OK to write up something, I'll tell you. If not, you'll keep your trap shut."

"And suppose I don't? You aren't going to try to threaten me, are you? You said yourself that you don't go in for murder."

Don Weatherbee smiled. "No threats. You could go ahead and do as you please. You could even go to Dalton now and tell him what I said. But I don't advise it."

I got out of the car. "May I ask why not?"

"Glad you did." He started up the motor again and closed the door. "Told you I was tied up with the White Brotherhood, remember? Well, your little stranger sounds to me like one of our boys. I don't know him—wish I did, because he might have the answers—but I know a couple more like him. Nice, clean, Godfearing citizens, but a bit on the fanatical side. Open to suggestions, too, if you catch my meaning. I think some of them carry knives, same as the character you met. And if I slipped them the word that you were an enemy of the Brotherhood, that maybe you had something to do with the fire and the murder of Amos Peabody—"

He chuckled. "No threats, understand. Just something to think about. Run along, Dempster, and write a good story. I'll be seeing you about the other story tomorrow."

I went inside and opened the door of my apartment. It took quite a while, because my hand was trembling so I couldn't control the key.

12

IT ISN'T easy to tell it this way—about how my hand trembled, about being afraid. Not after a steady diet of magazines and movies and TV, where every man is a Private Eye winking at danger.

I sat in my apartment, trying to write the inquest story for Cronin, and I kept thinking about the set-up. A Private Eye wouldn't have muffed things. If a Private Eye had taken the knife from my clown-faced friend, he'd have given him a clout on the head in return—and probably snapped a couple of wrists in the bargain.

If a Private Eye had Agatha Loodens where I had her last night, he'd have hung on to her until he got everything he wanted, and that doesn't necessarily just mean information.

If a Private Eye had been threatened by Weatherbee now, he'd know what to do. Private Eyes always know what to do. They may get sapped, slugged, shot and tortured, but that doesn't seem to matter. They keep right on going, day and night, without any sleep and with only rye for nourishment. And apparently they tap some source of cosmic energy—maybe they use VITAL CREAM. Whatever it is, they're always ready for a fight with a fiend or a bout with a blonde. To top it off, they also know all the answers. The best one can apparently solve any crime in 26 minutes flat, leaving plenty of time for four full minute commercials. Good deal.

The only trouble was that my name happened to be Phil Dempster. I wasn't a Private Eye, merely a private citizen. I didn't know who set those fires, who killed Peabody or Ricardi. And I was scared.

I pecked out a few lines on the story, then called Schwarm. Right now I was ready for a nice, long talk. "You asked me if I had any personal problems, Doc," I'd say. "Well, if you can come over, maybe I can answer that one for you."

That's what I'd say, what I intended to say. But there was no answer.

I hunted up his home phone, called. All I got was the ringing in the ears. Even that was better than nothing, better than silence. I held the phone for a long time, not wanting to lose the sound of the ring.

Silence was getting on my nerves. Maybe I ought to move to a noisier place. A place where there'd be people all around me. A place where Mrs. Loodens and the clown-faced cultist and Don Weatherbee couldn't find me. A place the killer wouldn't know about.

I thought about that for a moment. Then I thought about calling Captain Dalton. That made sense. I could tell him Weatherbee had threatened me. He'd given me police protection. Nobody could touch me, then.

But how long would that last? How long would the cops furnish me with a free bodyguard—a week, ten days? Suppose they found the firebug sooner? That would end my protection. And Weatherbee would wait. He was a big man in town, he had standing, a reputation. He'd deny any threats, maybe he'd even sue me. And when something finally happened to me, who could prove anything?

Something would happen to me sooner or later. I believed that. Weatherbee warned me it would, if I went to the cops.

That made sense, too.

So there was nothing to do now except go back to the typewriter and pound out my thousand words on the inquest. I had to make four false starts before I got going, and it was after three when I finished.

But nobody interrupted me. Nobody came to shove a knife in my ribs or a gun in my back.

I put the story in my pocket, locked the place up, and drove downtown. I stopped off long enough for a quick bite, then walked in on Cronin.

"Here's the inquest yarn," I said.

"Good." He read it over. I picked up the paper and read the *Globe* account. All very straight stuff. But I noted that Dalton had issued a statement following the inquest, and so had the District Attorney. The case wasn't closed. The inquest was merely a formality, absolving previous suspects. The person or persons responsible for the crimes would be apprehended by the Department. And so on.

"This is all right." Cronin waved my story at me. "Wish you'd been here a little earlier, though. Your friend Schwarm is down at headquarters, looking over the day's haul. The boys have been out with their butterfly nets. There's a lot of cross-examining going on."

"Maybe I'll look in tonight," I said.

"You'd better. We'll want another yarn for Monday, unless they manage to snag their man."

"Think they'll get him?"

Cronin lifted his eyebrows. "Who knows? Ninety percent of these cases break only because somebody tips the police off. It's that way all over the country. If the average guy knew how many thousands of unsolved murders have been committed, how many killers are running around loose, he'd be surprised. And scared silly."

"I'm a little scared myself," I said.

His eyes narrowed. "Anybody try to pressure you?" he asked.

"No," I said slowly. But I couldn't resist fishing. "Only there's angles here I don't get. Mrs. Loodens talked to me. So did Don Weatherbee."

"Give you any information?"

I shook my head. "They were asking, not telling."

"Well, that's only natural. Everybody's antsy about this thing." He stood up. "Phil, I hope something happens soon to crack this business. It could be bad."

"How do you mean?"

"Remember last year, when they caught this kid carving up his girl-friend?"

"Miller, wasn't it?"

"That's the name. Well, within the next two weeks, there were six more cases like it. People playing sex-maniac. Something seems to set off a wave. All of the perverts and offbeats in town read about those crimes and get ideas."

"Think there'll be more fires, Ed?"

He nodded. "I know it. Matter of fact, they've started already."

"You serious?"

"Running the story tomorrow. Since Ricardi's death the Fire Department has answered twenty-six alarms in two days. The average is eight."

"Anything big?"

"No. Lucky so far. But they're all alike, and that's the point. Crank jobs. Amateur torch works. Fires in baby carriages—empty ones,

154

thank God. Fires in alleys, in hallways, in places where there should be no fires. Kids started most of them."

"That's what Schwarm said," I told him. "Most firebugs are adolescents."

"Never mind the psychology," Cronin muttered. "Save it for the stories. But I'm worried. There's a real firebug still at large. And your little pal with the big knife."

I grinned, in spite of myself.

"What's so funny?" he asked.

"Nothing. Just glad to find out I'm not the only one who's scared about all this. But I never figured you'd feel that way."

Cronin gave me a long look. "I know," he said. "Anybody in the newspaper business knows. We get a lot of stories, and we don't run 'em all. And what we do run, we tone down. But we end up with a little different slant on people. I mentioned unsolved murders before. That's only a small part of it. This city—every town, every community—is filled with secrets. Two million abortions reported a year, and who knows how many unreported? Thirty thousand people disappear—a hundred a day, year in and year out. Just disappear, never heard of again. That's bad enough.

"Your friend with the shiv isn't exactly a news-items to us. There's probably five million just like him, and another five million who carry guns. Not professional criminals, but screwballs. The kind who need treatment, need to be put away."

He walked over to the window and leaned against the dirty glass. A big man staring thoughtfully down at his city spread out below him. You work for a paper as long as Cronin had and you wind up married to the city. You chart her progress and take her temperature now and then and when she gets sick, you worry about her. Now Cronin knew she was incubating a virulent disease and he was concerned. It was a side of the man I always suspected was there but one he seldom displayed.

"If you only knew what's going on out there," he said slowly. "If you only knew how many of the citizens are psychos. Doc Schwarm could probably make a guess—I've heard it said that one person out of three needs psychiatric treatment at some time or other in the course of a lifetime. And how many actually get it? Damned few. So we've got a city full of offbeats. People who walk around talking to themselves. People who sleep with guns under their pillows because they're afraid somebody is out to get them. People who make homemade bombs, who poison dogs, who chain their kids or their wives up in attics. Rapists. Rippers. Guys who go after women with whips and razor-blades. Homos. The stories I've heard, the things I've seen in the last ten years— nobody likes to think about them, nobody likes to believe them, but they're all true. People are naturally vicious."

"People are afraid," I said. "That's the answer. Fear makes them cruel. Sometimes they're afraid of things that aren't real. Sometimes they put their faith into things that aren't real either. That's why they join these cults."

"Cults!" Cronin spat the world. "I'd like to smash every damned one of them. I'd like to stamp out every phoney freak setup in the world—every racket that thrives on and encourages maladjustment. Only one good thing has come of this so far; the White Brotherhood and the Golden Atom setups are gone. Maybe that's what this firebug has in mind. Maybe he plans to burn out every cult in town."

I looked at Cronin. He was shaking with rage.

"You sound a little fanatical yourself," I said quietly. "Do you really mean that?"

"Of course I do. I know what goes on. For two years my wife was mixed up with some damned fake healing outfit—nobody could talk her out of it. Until her appendix ruptured and she almost died. Lost our baby on account of it. And fed a fortune to those charlatans. I hate the scum!"

"Well." I stood up. "Better run along."

Cronin sighed and wearily wiped his forehead. "Sorry I blew up that way," he said. "Pay no attention to me. Been a hard week."

"Sure."

"You'll try to find out what Schwarm did with these suspects?"

"Have a story for you Monday," I promised. "Take care of yourself."

I went out. I went out and ate and thought over the interview. Everybody was a screwball or a potential screwball, according to Cronin. And Cronin hated cults, wanted to see them burn. He'd given me this assignment to expose cults.

Where had *he* been during the fires? What kind of a potential did he have?

But that was crazy. Cronin couldn't be the firebug. He was just a normal guy—but one out of three needs psychiatric treatment sooner or later, and how many of them get it?

I ate at the Dinner Gong, and the toast was burned. *Burned.* In an hour, I was due at the Temple of the Living Flame. I didn't want to go there. I hadn't told Cronin I was going tonight. Weatherbee didn't want anyone to know.

I thought about the Temple of the Living Flame. Weatherbee had told me it was a firebug hangout, and that sounded logical. A natural, in fact. Why hadn't the police looked into this?

Come to think of it, maybe my notebook would give me a little advance information. I was supposed to see a man named Ogundu. Foreign-sounding name. Polish, or Russian, perhaps.

It was seven o'clock. I had just time enough to take a run back to the apartment, pick up the notebook, and be on my way. On my not-so-merry way.

I drove swiftly. I parked two doors down

from my place, then headed for the door. Somebody honked a horn at me.

"Mr. Dempster!"

I turned, recognizing the voice. I recognized the car, too. There she was again, waiting for me.

"Hello," I said. "Still mad?"

She shook her head. The blonde hair was worn in an upsweep tonight, and the earrings were pendant.

"Aren't you going to ask me up?" she inquired.

"Sorry. I've got an appointment."

"I wanted to talk to you."

"Stick around," I said. "Got to get something. Be right down."

It didn't take more than two minutes. I went up, pocketed the notebook, and came out to her car. She opened the door for me. I climbed in and sat down.

Agatha Loodens seemed to be all set for a big evening. I couldn't help but take a good look at her, and there was plenty for me to see tonight. I'm not talking about the jewelry or the fancy hairdo, either; just her own dainty, demure, *décolleté* self. She looked like she'd been poured into her dress by somebody whose hand wasn't quite steady.

My hand wouldn't have been steady, either. I sat next to her now, staring at the cleavage.

"I had hoped to speak to you after the inquest," she told me. "But you left so quickly. With Mr. Weatherbee."

"That's right."

"What did he want?"

"Nothing. Just talked a little about the case."

"Phil—I meant what I said last night. Keep away from the man. He's dangerous." She paused. "Very."

"I'm being careful these days." I paused. "Very." Then I stopped watching the double-feature long enough to look her in the eye. "Is that what you came here to see me about?"

"Please. I'm not just snooping. When I saw you go out with Don this noon, I got worried."

"Why? Afraid he'd tell me something I shouldn't know?"

Her lips tightened. "Must you be such a—?"

"Don't say it." I grinned. "Sorry, but I guess I must. Too many people keep coming at me these days. All of them are warning me, and none of them really give a damn about me."

"Are you sure?"

She was very close, and her lips weren't tight any more. They were loose, and full, and I could see the tip of her tongue, like a little pink doormat with the word *Welcome* on it.

"I'm not sure of anything," I said.

"Must you keep that appointment?" she murmured.

"Yes."

"Is it with Weatherbee?"

"No. I'm not seeing him tonight."

"Good. I found out a few things about him today. Things you'd be interested in knowing."

"Such as?"

"He's got another cult, Phil. He's mixed up with that White Brotherhood gang."

"I already know that. He told me himself."

"But there's more to it, Phil. A lot more. Things he wouldn't tell you. I'm sure of it. If you'd only listen to me, let me help you—"

"You can." I sat up and moved away. "I'll be through with my chores by eleven. How about stopping back here then? We'll have all the time we want."

Agatha Loodens nodded. Then she leaned over and her mouth met mine. It was a cordial meeting, and I hated to break it up, but I had to. "See you at eleven," I said.

"Yes. And—take care of yourself."

"Now she tells me." I waved, and she drove away. I waited until the car rounded the corner and disappeared, then walked over to my own heap. I climbed in and opened the notebook.

Here was the stuff on the Brotherhood, the Golden Atom, Wisdom Center, House of Truth, New Kingdom Tabernacle, and—nothing.

I riffled through the pages again. I found the Temple of the Living Flame listed up front, with its address opposite the entry, and the name Ogundu beneath. But there was no inner heading, no additional notes. Apparently Cronin's people hadn't gotten around to this one.

Or had they? And had someone gotten around to them?

I shrugged. Things were getting out of hand. Now I was really letting my imagination run away with me. Figuring Cronin for a firebug, seeing a man hiding under every bed. A man with a knife and a torch.

Time to stop. And time to go. I put the car in gear and drove to 101 South Sherburne Street and the Temple of the Living Flame.

13

IT WAS my night for surprises.

The setting was no surprise. The Negro ghetto on the South Side. The night was hot and muggy and the odors from the cheap and dirty restaurants clung close to the pavement. Greasy ham and eggs, black-eyed peas, turnip greens—a rich mixture for a queasy nose. The no-down-payment-and-the-rest-of-your-life-to-pay furniture stores stuffed with upholstered borax in purple and orange and black, the inevitable auto agency selling long, black Lincolns, a cut-rate drug-store, the usual combination package-liquor store and bar, a former dance hall turned roller skating rink. . . . The placid black faces that filled the walk, the rumble of the elevated overhead.

A cool wind blew off the lake and for no good reason at all I reflected that it would probably be a night like this on which I'd die. Alone and overlooked, with life buzzing quietly on about me. Just so long as I could never see myself with the flesh beginning to redden and char, the eyes start ...

I blotted it out and parked across the street from the small, two-storey white frame building, sitting in the car and studying the setup for a moment. It looked like any one of half a dozen churches you can find in colored neighborhoods—a former store, converted into a mission or a tabernacle, its windows covered by heavy drapes. Over the doorway was a sign, illuminated by a large outdoor bulb. TEMPLE OF THE LIVING FLAME—ALL WELCOME. It was the doorway which furnished the surprise.

Because now, as I watched, out of it marched a familiar figure. I recognized the pipe-in-jaw profile of Captain Dalton. He was followed by two other plain-clothes men. They went down the block to a waiting car, got in, drove off.

So they *had* got around to this place after all! Perhaps my visit was unnecessary. Even so, duty called. Duty—and Don Weatherbee.

I sat in the car a while longer. It wasn't quite eight yet. There'd be time to watch the early arrivals. Might be some one worth seeing.

That's what I told myself. Actually, I knew who I was looking for. I didn't want to see him, but he might show up. My little clown-faced apparition.

They were coming to the meeting now, and so far I hadn't spotted the man I was searching for. Most of the faces weren't even white. That was another surprise. What was I getting into now—an old-fashioned Revival Meeting?

I got out and went over. People were still going into the place, and now I saw that they weren't all Negroes. There was a little man with a twisted arm who tipped his cap to me as he passed; a thin, almost rachitic girl with pale yellow hair; an elderly bum with a milk-white cast covering his left eye; several teen-agers in the regulation uniform of leather jacket and blue-jeans; an unshaven drunk; a well-dressed young woman in heavy makeup; three beat types, two with crewcuts and the third with a macro- or hydrocephalic bulge which needed no tonsorial garnish to attract attention.

A strange assortment. Or was it? Hadn't Schwarm told me about firebugs? Adolescents, the physically deformed, the subnormal and abnormal? If these *were* firebugs. I had Weatherbee's word for that.

Half past eight. Time to go in. I walked up the steps, opened the door.

The lobby entry was small. No comparison here with the splash of the Church of the Golden Atom. No tables offering written or bottled guarantees of eternal youth. It was just an alcove, leading directly into the Temple.

The Temple had folding chairs arranged in rows before a small platform. The walls were

165

draped in heavy monks-cloth, but the general effect was that of a cheap auction-house.

Only the backdrop of the stage was indicative of the purpose and activities of this organization. The heavy, black drapes hung from ceiling to floor, completely covering the wall or whatever was behind them. And sewn in the center, with threads of flame, was the vivid outline of a burning bird. It was a simple symbol, but subtly compelling—and I recognized what it represented. The Phoenix, the resurrection bird that rises anew from its own ashes.

Suddenly the firebird shivered and split asunder. A man had parted the drapes in the middle and stepped forth on the platform. Ogundu—and another surprise.

I really should have expected it. He wouldn't be Polish or Russian. He was a Negro, slender and splendid, black as the night in a robe as red as living flame.

He stood there, theatrically poised, hands uplifted, and the crowd rose to its feet. There were deacons present now, I noted. One of them stood at the far wall, ready to switch out the lights, and I wondered if the Temple held its meetings in darkness. Then I noted two others, each on either side of the platform altar. They carried candles which they held over large pot-like objects which stood on tripods. Now I knew their purpose. The pots were braziers.

Ogundu's hands came down. "Kindle the Living Flame!" he said.

And from all around me came the response. "Kindle the Living Flame!" It was a chant, a ritual.

The candles dipped. The lights flicked off and the fires flared up—flared from the braziers to flood Ogundu's face and send shimmering shadows across the figure of the Phoenix.

I sat there and stared. I'd admired Professor Ricardi's pitch, his smooth performance in the fancy auditorium with the organ offering accompaniment. He'd used all the trimmings to get the crowd worked up.

But he hadn't got to me. Even after the full treatment, I'd still remained an aloof, objective observer.

This was different.

I felt something crawl up into my throat.

Oh, I knew what was happening. I knew I was sitting in a dingy little converted store in a dingy little district, surrounded by a crowd of credulous cretins. I knew that Ogundu was as big a fake as Ricardi—his ebony was just as phoney as Ricardi's gold.

But he was doing something to me in spite of all I realized. This nondescript Negro in a rented theatrical costume had taken a few yards of velvet, a couple of candles, and some second-hand smudge-pots, switched off the lights, and made a Mystery.

What had Schwarm said? Something I already knew, something everybody knows. *Fire is magic.* Ogundu brought fire, and he was Prometheus and Pythagoras and Zoroaster and Mazda and Ahriman—all the gods and devils and wonder-workers incarnate.

The crowd stirred restlessly, watching the flames. I knew why they came here, now. Fire was the lure. Fire that burns, fire that destroys, fire that creates, fire that purifies, fire that is living death and death-in-life.

Ogundu was talking now. He had a deep baritone voice, the voice of the evangelist, the voice of the prophet, the voice of the sayer of sooth. There have always been such voices, there have always been men who kindled an altar-flame before which men gathered to look, to listen, and to learn. Learn the secret of Fire which is Being, which is Magic.

Some of this was my thought, some of it was Ogundu's words.

He wasn't preaching, in the usual meaning of the term. He wasn't exhorting or explaining, he wasn't promising boons or blessings, selling salve or offering unguent. He was proclaiming the true God—the Living Flame. The Flame men must willingly worship to escape destruction.

Fire is Life. Fire is Death. And Fire is also Hell. Those who do not worship will learn. Those who do not give themselves to the Flame will be given to It in Afterlife. For the World and the Universe was born of Fire, and we are all a part of it. That is the great secret—not to oppose the Truth.

He chanted the ancient, mystic words. Just so much gibberish, really. It's always gibberish when you remember it, write it down. But when you hear it in the dark, and the fire flares—real fire, that really burns—something happens.

I knew, now. Weatherbee was right, Schwarm was right, Cronin was right. The world is full of them: full of twisted bodies and twisted minds that feed on flame. I could feel them beside me in the darkness, catch glimpses of faces shining in the firelight. That's the way faces must shine in Hell. Red eyes, red teeth, red hands all about me. And the voice chanting, the breath panting, the urge rising in the room as the flames rose—the haunting wanting, the desire for fire, a burning yearning, flowing and glowing—

From out of nowhere the thought crept into my mind and it was like a voice crying *Save me, save me.* I recognized the voice, and thrust it down again; down into the dream where it belonged.

And I thrust again, burying it, and I thrust away the flame-born fancies. This was just another cheap, phoney little racket. In a minute they'd turn on the lights and pass the collection plate around. Get any group together, turn out the lights, kindle a fire and let somebody start using wizard's words in a deep voice; you're bound to get a reaction. No matter how sophisticated the group may be, the reaction will come.

Yes, but *why?* Was it because there really *is*
something about darkness and fire that means
magic? Is it atavistic, do we all go back to the
cave-dwellers who gathered around the flame
that kept back the blackness and its beasts? Do
we all have some hidden heritage from the
time when every temple guarded an altar of
the gods, when enemies were destroyed in a
holy holocaust? Was there an instinctive
reaction?

Whatever it was, I felt it now. I knew why
the others came here, knew why fire held a
fascination.

My throat was dry, swollen. My hands were
clenched, rigid at my sides, and my heart was
beginning to pound in rhythm with Ogundu's
baritone booming, in rhythm with the rise and
fall of the flames. This was it. *This is a how a
firebug feels before—*

Had I ever felt this way? In the past, in the
dim past, five days ago, when the White
Brotherhood tabernacle burned? Did I *know*
this feeling?

That was a crazy thought. Maybe all my
thoughts were crazy. Maybe nobody else here
felt like this. Or maybe I wasn't crazy, and
they all did—and if so, that was crazier still.

I snapped my attention back to the stage.
Something was happening on the platform
now. The deacons were up there. They were
bringing in this long box, this long, shallow
trough. It came from behind the curtains, and
so did the iron fire-pot. The iron fire-pot, with

its long handles—it took two men to lift it and bring it forward, smoking and hissing.

Ogundu was chanting something abut faith, now. The crowd responded. It was like a hymn without music, but it had a counterpoint. The hissing of hot coals, live coals.

The deacons dumped the fire-pot's contents into the long, shallow trough. It stretched halfway across the front of the platform, and sent a swirl of smoke up to veil Ogundu's face.

For a moment it seemed like a Revival Meeting once again. The shrill shrieks of Negro women, the grunting affirmations of the men rose all about me. I'd heard cries like that before, from those possessed of the Spirit.

Possession. Demoniac possession. Demon of fire.

I told myself that my name was Philip Dempster, that I was sitting in a remodelled store, watching a cult racketeer put on a show. But somehow the message didn't get through to my throat and hands and lungs and heart. The pulsing and pounding, the rigor and rictus went on.

And I watched as Ogundu ripped the enfolding flame from his body, cast off the crimson robe, and stood before us in the firelight, stripped to the waist. He stopped and flung his shoes aside.

He closed his eyes. The four deacons chanted and he responded. Somebody began to stamp on the floor with both feet. In a moment the pounding rose all around me—the rhythmic,

measured stamping that's older than Stone-
henge. It made the floor vibrate, made the
flames quiver. I was vibrating and quivering
with them.

Ogundu moved barefoot to one end of the
trough. He moved swiftly, with feline grace, a
black panther. His eyes were embers. One of
the deacons handed him a vial, and he dipped
into it and tossed something down into the
long, shallow trough before him. The coals
hissed and sputtered, sizzled and seared as
smoke smouldered up anew.

And then Ogundu listened to the drumming,
listened to it well and swell. A moment he
stood there, and then he started forward.

He walked slowly, now—walked on naked
feet across the bed of live coals.

Then he walked back.

I'd read about it, of course. They say it's
done in Africa, by witch-doctors.

But this wasn't a case of what I read or what
they said. This wasn't Africa, and Ogundu
wasn't a witch-doctor. This was 101 South
Sherburne Street, right here, and I saw a man
walk barefoot over fire.

Sure, the lights came on, just as I knew they
would, and the deacons were only ordinary
Negroes in cheap suits, coming down the aisle
with the collection plates. And somebody was
spreading ashes on the fire, and then pouring
water—the braziers were extinguished, and
people were pushing back those battered folding chairs. The show was over.

Yet I'd seen something tonight. I remembered Seabrook's old book, *The Magic Island*,
and his account of Haiti. How the simple,
friendly, ignorant Negro farmers gathered together, and how the beating of a drum and the
summoning of the Snake transformed them
momentarily into a magic multitude, votaries
of Voodoo. Seabrook had sensed the summoning of a Mystery.

And I?

I wasn't sure. One thing I did know—this
time there wouldn't be any slip-ups. I intended
to see Ogundu, and see him right now.

Down the aisle, up onto the platform. One of
the deacons barred my way.

"Where you headin' for, Mister?"

"I want to see Ogundu."

"The Father has retired."

"I'm from the *Globe*." For the first time I was
glad Cronin had given me a press card. I pulled
it out but he didn't bother to read it.

"Wait. I'll tell him. What's your name,
Mister?"

"Philip Dempster. He'll probably know who I
am."

The deacon parted the curtains. He wasn't
gone long. When he emerged again, he was
smiling.

"You can go right back," he told me. "First
door down the hall."

I went right back.

Behind the curtains was a doorway leading

into the hall corridor. I found the first door, opened it.

This was what lay behind the black curtain of Mystery—this was what lurked behind the portals guarded by the Phoenix. Just an ordinary little office, filled with second-hand furniture. At first I was disappointed. Disappointed in the appearance of the place, and disappointed in the appearance of the thin, middle-aged Negro who sat beside the desk, soaking his naked feet in a dented tin basin.

"Got to soak this gunk off," he grinned. "Stuff sticks." He picked a cigar-butt from an ashtray on the desk. "Sit down," he invited. "How'd you like the show?"

I opened my mouth. Just then a girl stuck her head into the room—a white girl.

Ogundu turned and waved her away. "It's all right," he said. "I won't need you any more tonight."

She looked at me, nodded, and withdrew.

"My secretary," Ogundu told me. "Nice girl."

"Yeah," I nodded. "Nice girl." I stared at the doorway, trying to get a glimpse of the hall outside.

But Diana Rideaux had disappeared.

14

Ogundu dried his feet. I stared at the pink soles. There wasn't the slightest sign of a burn. I didn't see any callouses, either.

"What's the secret?" I asked. "Is it that preparation you smeared on?"

He smiled. "Partly. And part of it's the kind of coals—porous stuff, gives off heat as fast as it absorbs it. But the big thing is knowing how to walk, and not being afraid. Ever hear of the Nigerian Fire Walkers?"

"Don't tell me you're from Ghana?"

He shook his head. "Born and raised right here in town. But you don't have to go to Africa to learn a few tricks. I've got others. Fire-eating, and picking up red-hot pokers. They go for that kind of jazz in a big way around here."

"Aren't you afraid I'll quote you in my writeup?" I asked.

Ogundu chewed the end of his cigar. "Go ahead. It won't bother me any. You just got in on the last performance."

"You're quitting the Temple?"

"That right. As of now."

"Dalton scare you?"

"Told me to lay off, if that's what you mean. Said he'd have the Fire Marshal get after me for violating ordinances. Said I couldn't mess around with torches and live coals. He leaned on me pretty hard."

"What are your plans?"

"Cutting out of here right quick. Sell this place for whatever it'll bring."

"Then you don't care what I write?"

Ogundu shrugged. "Do as you please. By the time your story's out, I'll be on my way." He started to put on his stockings and shoes. "Anything you want to know about the gimmicks I use, just go ahead and ask."

"That's nice of you to be so cooperative," I told him. "I appreciate it."

"No sense being funky, the way I figure it." He laced his shoes slowly. "When you gotta go, you gotta go. I've had all I could expect here, anyway." He sat up, smiling. "Now, Mr. Dempster, what you want to know?"

I smiled back at him and took a deep breath. "I want to know if you have any firebugs in your congregation."

His smile melted away like butter on a hot

griddle. "What's that got to do with your newspaper story?"

"Plenty. I'm not so much interested in the cult angle any more. It's the firebug I'm after."

"You working with the cops?"

"No. Not officially. I'm working for myself. Twice now I've been involved in this series of cases. I don't like incendiaries and I don't like killers. I want to find out what this is all about."

"So does your friend Captain Dalton. Did you send him here, is that it?"

"Believe me, I had nothing to do with it. But it's only natural he'd come around. Knowing what you were doing here, running the kind of racket that is bound to attract every potential pyromaniac in town."

"I told you I'm getting out."

"Yes. But you haven't answered my question."

"I can't answer it, Mr. Dempster. I don't know the answer. You think if one of my people was a firebug, he'd tell me about it?" He paused. "Or do you maybe figure I trained a couple of them to start those fires on purpose? Is that it?"

"I don't think anything. I'm waiting to hear what you think."

"Far as I know, all my people are clean. But you don't have to take my word for it. Ask Captain Dalton. When he walked out of here earlier tonight, he had a list of every name I got in the files. Does that answer your question?"

"Partly," I said. I leaned forward. "Speaking

of your people, maybe you can give me some information. Does one of them happen to be a little man, about five feet three or four, who wears a brown topcoat? The one I'm thinking of is almost bald. He has a white face, deep circles under his eyes, and he's got a habit of biting his lips. Looks a little bit like a clown—"

Ogundu stood up. He walked over to the filing cabinet, opened it, took out an object and threw it on the desk. It clattered and lay still. I gazed down on the glittering length of a knife. I'd seen it before—felt its edge against my ribs.

"Does this belong to him?" Ogundu asked.

"Yes. You know him."

"I saw him last night. Worked late, and about ten o'clock I decided to go out for coffee. Just as I opened the side door, this came whizzing at me. Stuck in the door-frame just next to my right ear. I saw your little man then. He ran down the alley, but not before I got a good look. Who is he?"

"I don't know," I said. "But I want to. Did you tell the police?"

Ogundu shook his head. "Got enough troubles without that. Been like this all week, ever since that Brotherhood fire. People warning me somebody's out to get all us cult leaders. My secretary scared half to death, wanting to quit."

"Your secretary," I said. "What about her?"

"Nothing about her. Name's Rideaux. Diana Rideaux. Been with me six-seven months now. Good girl. Nice girl. You saw her."

I nodded. "Is she a—believer?"

"You mean does she go for this Living Flame line? No. She's got a head on her shoulders. How could she, when she knows all the tricks? Why do you ask?"

"Just wondering. After all, it's rather unusual to find a—I mean, a job like this—"

Ogundu smiled again. "I know what you mean. She's a white girl working for a Negro. Well, I can give you the answer to that one. It's a hundred bucks a week. That's all. But Diana's worth it, she's sensible. Or was, up until this week. Lately she's had all kinds of notions about being followed. Come to think of it, she said something about this little guy with the knife. That was on Thursday, I guess. I laughed at her."

"You aren't laughing now."

"That's right. I'm not laughing. I'm leaving."

"You're scared," I murmured.

"All right. I'm scared. I had me a sweet little setup here, no trouble. And all of a sudden things start happening. Bad things. Fires and killings and people coming on strong with knives. I don't know what it's all about and I don't want to find out. Go ahead and print it in the paper if you like—print it that I'm scared and running away. I don't care."

"You'd like that, wouldn't you?" I said. "Having people think you left town because you're frightened. Instead of having them think you left because you know too much."

"I don't know anything," Ogundu said.

"I wish you'd tell me. Maybe I could help. You don't want to see this sort of thing go on, do you? Innocent people being murdered, a whole city in danger—"

"I helped all I could," he answered. "Now's the time to cut out."

It seemed like good advice. I took it. "Good night," I said.

"Goodbye."

I walked through the deserted Temple and out to the street. The little man wasn't waiting for me there, and he wasn't waiting for me at the car. It wouldn't have startled me too greatly if he had been. This was my night for surprises.

But he wasn't surprising me. I drove home quickly, noting that it was already a few minutes past eleven.

I parked out in front and looked around for Mrs. Loodens and her car. Apparently she hadn't arrived yet. Just to make sure I went upstairs. My door was locked and she wasn't in the hall.

I came back down again and waited in the lobby. The minutes crawled past. Eleven fifteen, eleven thirty, eleven forty.

Apparently that was the last surprise of the evening. For some reason or other, she wasn't coming.

I turned to go back up the stairs when the taxi pulled up in front of the lobby door. I watched it deposit the final surprise on the curb.

Diana Rideaux came up the walk, opened the door, and stepped right into my arms.

15

WE LAY on the sofa. Quite a bit of time had gone by, and Mrs. Loodens hadn't showed up. I didn't have a light burning for her in the window. In fact, I didn't have any light at all.

"Feel better now?" I whispered.

"Um-hum."

"But why didn't you tell me?"

"What? About working for Ogundu? How could I, after what you said about cults, people who ran them? I was ashamed—" She moved away. "I'm ashamed right now."

I moved her back.

"But you came here anyway."

"I had to. When I saw you at the Temple tonight, I knew it was something I had to do. I wasn't afraid any more."

"You know I'd never hurt you," I said.

"Yes. I was a fool, letting myself think that—"

"Think what?"

The words were whispers. "I thought you were the firebug."

"Because of that business with the cigarette the other night? That was an accident."

"Yes." She sighed. "Only at the time, I wasn't sure. And then I read about Professor Ricardi in the papers."

"But you must have read my alibi, too, and what they said at the inquest."

She pressed close again. "I'm sorry. It's just that I've been so worried. And then when I was followed—"

"Who followed you?"

"Please. It's nothing. Ogundu said I was imagining things."

"Did you see who it was? Could it have been a little white-faced man?"

"I didn't actually see anyone." She clung and whispered. "Besides, it doesn't matter now. Nobody can hurt me when I'm with you, can they, Phil? You aren't angry because of what I thought, you forgive me—"

"There's nothing to forgive. You're not the only one who doubted my story. And I've been running around suspecting everybody. Including you, when you popped into the doorway of Ogundu's office." I smoothed her hair. "But it's all right now. I don't give a damn who you work for, as long as you're my girl."

"I am your girl, Phil. You know that."

"Yes."

"And I'm quitting Ogundu."

"Good idea." Apparently he hadn't told her about his plans for leaving town. And I didn't think this was the time or place to mention it. Still, I couldn't resist doing a little probing.

"Diana, when I talked to Ogundu tonight I questioned him about the fires. I wondered if some of his followers could be involved. You know the setup—what do you think?"

She sat up, suddenly thoughtful. "I never saw anything suspicious. They get pretty worked up at those meetings, but nothing's ever happened that I know about. Even at the brandings—"

"What brandings? Ogundu didn't mention that."

"Some of the deacons, the Inner Circle, they call themselves, go through a ritual. They have the brand of the Phoenix burned on their arms or chests."

"Sounds pretty barbaric."

"That's what I thought, too. But Ogundu says it's nothing; they even do it in fraternities, sometimes. Just sucker stuff, he calls it."

I squeezed her hand. "What kind of a man is Ogundu, anyway?" I kept my voice calm. "What are his habits? Does he have any special foibles or eccentricities?"

Her hand trembled, pulled away. "Phil, is *that* it? Do you think *he* might—?"

"I don't know."

"It's like a nightmare, isn't it?" she whispered. "Everywhere you turn, there's something lurking."

"Take it easy," I said. I pulled her back down beside me on the sofa. "Stop trembling. I won't hurt you."

"I know. But when I think about what's happened—please, Phil, turn on the light."

"Afraid of the dark?" I bent my head. Her mouth twisted free of mine.

"Afraid of *me?*" I had to say it, had to hear her answer. I waited for it. And it came, but not in words; only in a trembling silence that was worse than words.

I could feel her body beneath me, feel my arms holding her just as I'd held her before. Just the way I'd held Ricardi when I turned his body over and saw his face. Just the way I held the *other* body in my dreams, when I turned it over and saw its face, saw the bubbling eyes, the burned mask. I'd seen it in my dreams and I knew what it was. But I couldn't tell Dalton, I couldn't tell Schwarm, I was even afraid to tell myself.

That's why I drank, so I could sleep without the dream; but sooner or later I'd have to tell. Have to separate the dream from the reality, have to know where one left off and the other began.

But not yet. I couldn't face it now. I couldn't face the face. Drinking was better, and *this* was better. Yes, this was better. I held her now, and I could go on and forget again for a little while.

"Stop!" she whimpered.

Only I didn't stop, because if I stopped I'd remember, and that was too much to bear. *Pyrophobia*, Schwarm had guessed, and he had guessed the truth. Fear of fire. Fear of remembering a fire and a face.

I held her, and my hand went to the top of her dress, and she whimpered again but I was going on, I had to go on, and then—

She wrenched her arm free and switched on the lamp.

It flared up, the light flared up, like fire.

I held her in my arms, staring down at the charred countenance of my dreams. Then I screamed.

"Margery!"

An instant. Only an instant, and then it was all right. The face was gone. Diana lay in my arms, sobbing. And now I could tell her, could tell her everything. I had to tell her so that she'd understand.

"It happened while I was out on the Coast," I whispered. "About a year ago. I was getting material for my book, and I met this girl. Her name was Margery Hunter. She was an artist, lived in a beach cottage south of Long Beach. We seemed to hit if off together right away. I wanted to marry her, but she made me promise to wait until the book was done and accepted.

"I finished the book and sent if off. Two months later it came back for minor revisions— but the publisher accepted it. So we held a party at her place, to celebrate. And announced our engagement.

"She had a lot of beat friends; artists, musicians, beach bums. They really believed in living it up. When we told them the reason for the party, they decided to make a night of it. One of them went out and brought back half a case of gin. Everybody got high, and I guess the party turned into a brawl.

"Margery passed out and we put her in the bedroom on the bed. The rest of us went right on drinking. Gradually most of the guests drifted off. There were only four of us left when Oscar—Oscar Ringold, the painter—suggested we go for a swim. That sounded good to everybody, so we went down to the beach and swam. The water sobered us up. When we came out we knew what we were doing. That's when Oscar called our attention to the lights in the cottage.

"You can probably figure out the rest. How the fire started, no one really knows to this day. Somebody must have dropped a cigarette. Just one of those accidents, one of those things you're always reading about.

"Only I wasn't reading about it this time. I was seeing it. There'd been a heavy wind off the ocean, and the fire had a head start. All it needed was a few minutes. By the time we got there, the flimsy little frame cottage was half gone—the whole roof caught at once, and the front door caved in.

"Margery was inside. Somebody ran up the

road to hail a car. Oscar and another man held me, but I broke loose. There was no way of getting in through the door, but I found the bedroom window and crawled inside.

"And I found Margery. She'd gotten up, of course, and tried to get out, but she never made it. Nobody could have made it through that heat. She was lying face down on the floor when I reached her, and I guess I got her outside in less than a minute. Even so, my clothes were burned, and my hair and eyebrows singed off. Margery's clothes were burned, too. But that wasn't all.

"I found that out when I carried her outside. It was bright as day now, with the flames leaping all around me, and I could see everything. I turned her over, and I saw what had happened to her face—that red, grisly mass, with the oozing eyes—"

I took a deep breath. "Something happened to me when I saw that face, Diana. They said I was in shock for two days: by the time I came around, everything was over. The cottage was gone, Margery was gone. They—they cremated her. After the inquest, of course."

"Were you accused?"

"There was no question of accusation. We were all held equally responsible—or irresponsible. Just a tragic accident, the papers called it. But I knew. It could have been my cigarette, don't you see? The way it was at the beach the other night. It could have been me. And if you'd seen her face and heard her—"

"Heard her?" Diana whispered.

"Yes. That's the worst. I didn't even remember *that* until I found Ricardi's body Thursday evening. I carried him out and turned him over. And when I looked at him it seemed for a moment as if I was back there, looking at Margery and hearing the voice coming, faint and faraway, from that burned mouth. The voice moaning, 'Save me, save me!' That's all she said. Because she died then, died in my arms."

I stood up. My shirt was soaked with sweat. "Now do you understand why I'm afraid?" I asked. "Why I drink, why I was drinking the other night? It's so I wouldn't have the dreams, so I could forget."

Margery came over to me and put her arms around me and I stared down into that ruined mask, and then it melted away and I knew I was holding Diana in my arms. Everything melted away.

"It's all right now," I murmured. And I meant it. It *was* all right. I'd talked it out.

"You're better than Schwarm," I told her.

"Not afraid any more?"

"No. Are you?"

She shook her head. "It's just that I didn't know."

I smiled at her. "Things are going to be better from now on," I said. "You'll see."

The phone rang.

I picked it up, answered, listened.

"You alone?" said the voice.

I hesitated a moment. "Yes. Why?"

"Come right down then. I just had a visitor. Your friend with the white face."

"Is he there now?"

"Took off like a bat out of hell. But not before he told me."

"Told you what?"

"What you're trying to find out, Dempster. That's why he came. Said he wanted to warn me I was next. And he knows who."

"Aren't you going to tell me?"

"When you come down. We can talk about the reward, then."

"What reward?" I asked.

"Paper said something about a thousand dollars. I could use that."

"I'll call my friend Cronin. He'll—"

"You call nobody. I don't want your friend Cronin. I don't want the cops messing around, either. I'm running like a thief. Catch me the six o'clock flight in the morning. So it's now or never."

"I'm on my way."

"Good. I'll be waiting. But no funny business. Come alone."

"Thanks."

I hung up.

Diana stood at my side. "Who was that?"

"Ogundu," I said. "I told you things would be better. He knows the identity of the firebug."

"What? But how—"

"My pal," I grinned. "My buddy. Clown-face. He came and warned him just now. I've got to get down there right away, because Ogundu's planning on leaving town."

"Aren't you going to call the police?"

"He made me promise not to. Your boss is a pretty frightened man."

Diana put her hand on my arm. "Why should he tell you? And what makes you believe his story about the little man?"

"Seems as if he'd like that thousand-dollar reward," I answered. "That's why he's willing to talk. And that business about the little man sounds convincing. After all, he seemed to know when Ricardi's number was up."

"Yes, but—"

"Come on," I said. "I've got to hurry. I'll drop you off at your place."

"Please, Phil. Don't take the chance."

"I've got to take it." I smiled at her. "I'll leave you at your apartment and go on alone. If I'm not back in half an hour, then you can call the cops. Good enough?"

She shook her head. "I'm going with you."

"He'll be sore."

"Don't worry about him. After all, he was going to run off without telling me, wasn't he? I'd show up Monday and find him gone. I don't owe him anything.

"Is that any reason for taking a chance?"

"Then you admit it might be dangerous." Diana smiled triumphantly. "All the more reason for me to go. From now on you aren't getting into any more messes unless you take me with you."

I shrugged. "All right. But you wait outside in the car."

"We'll talk about that when we get there. Come on."

Out the door, down the stairs. It was good to feel her arm under mine, but when we reached the lobby I broke free and went on ahead.

"Phil, what's the matter?"

"Nothing. Just checking." I flattened myself against the wall and peered through the glass door, scanning the street outside.

I'd thought I'd caught a glimpse of it passing as we came down the stairs, and I was right. It stood there now, parked at the curb—the big, black shiny new Lincoln.

"Come on," I murmured. "Out the back way, quick!"

She turned and started down the hall. I took one last look to make sure.

One last look, but it was enough. I saw Weatherbee emerge from the car and start toward the door. And he saw me. One hand went to his pocket, emerged. I moved away, quickly—but not quickly enough.

He ran. I looked over my shoulder. Diana was opening the back door at the other end of the hall. I watched her disappear, then turned to face the two of them—Weatherbee and his gun.

|16

"WHERE IS SHE?" Weatherbee gestured with the gun.

"Who?"

"You know who I'm talking about. What are you two trying to pull, anyway?"

"Nothing," I said. "We were just talking."

"Talking!" He moved closer. I could tell he'd been drinking, but his hand never wavered. "In the dark?"

"What's it to you? She's my girl."

"Oh, so she's *your* girl now, is she? You're a fast operator, Dempster. I got a good notion to slow you down."

"Hold on," I muttered. "You're all mixed up. You think I've been with Mrs. Loodens, is that it?"

"Think? I damned well know it."

"I did see her at seven, yes. But she drove away—hasn't come back. The girl I had upstairs just now was Diana Rideaux."

"Prove it."

"I can't. She just sneaked out the back."

"Let's go."

The gun prodded me through the exit. We stood alone in the area behind the apartment.

"She's gone," I said. "Nobody here now."

As I spoke the words, I realized the truth. There was nobody here. We were all alone in the darkness and nobody could help me. The night wind blew through the empty area-way. It would blow across the city, fanning the flames. It would blow through the hole in my skull when he pulled the trigger.

But he hadn't pulled the trigger, yet.

"I hope to God you're telling the truth," Weatherbee said. "There's nothing to gain, protecting a woman like Mrs. Loodens. I should have turned her in myself when I found out about her husband."

I blinked. "But she told me that—"

"Sure. She said I killed him. Don't be childish. Why should I do a thing like that, what would I gain? *She* inherited."

"Can you prove what you're saying?" I asked.

"You mean legal proof, evidence? No. If I could, I'd go to the police. But I'm going to nail her on this arson stuff, wait and see! Why do you think I've been tailing her all week?"

"Surely you don't believe she set the fires? Why should she burn the White Brotherhood tabernacle?"

"She knew I was his new partner and that scared her. She was afraid I'd take the play away from her and Ricardi. She set the fire. Simple."

"And then killed her own boy-friend? It doesn't make sense."

Weatherbee nodded slowly, but the gun never moved an inch. "I got news for you," he said. "Ricardi was getting ready to sell out to me. I had the deal all arranged. In a couple of weeks he would have announced a merger with the White Brotherhood."

"Did she know that?"

"He must have let something slip out. So she let him have it." He nodded again. "It figures, Dempster. You heard the evidence at the inquest. Nobody broke into Ricardi's place—he let the killer in himself. Who's the most logical person to get into Ricardi's bedroom late at night?"

"But her maid said she was home with a headache—"

"For twenty bucks she could get that girl to say anything."

I stared at him. "Are you sure this isn't just a case of jealousy?"

The gun jumped up and I gulped. I could see his fat forefinger squeeze down on the trigger. It squeezed, and then it relaxed. Weatherbee sighed.

"All right. I'm jealous. You saw her—you ought to be able to understand. But I know she's in on this, and I'm waiting for her."

"Well, she's not coming back tonight, apparently. I told you the truth—I was with Diana Rideaux, Ogundu's secretary."

"Ogundu's secretary?" The gun jumped up. "Why didn't you tell me that before?"

"You didn't give me a chance." I stared at the gun. "I met her the other night, but I didn't know she was working for Ogundu. I saw her again tonight, at his Temple, when I talked to him."

"What did he say?"

"He's leaving town. Frightened of the police, I guess."

"Does the girl know anything? Where were you two headed when you came downstairs just now?"

I hesitated.

Weatherbee's mouth tightened. So did his finger on the trigger.

"All right," I murmured. "We got a call from Ogundu. He's found out who the firebug is. I was going to talk to him now, before he left."

"What about the girl?"

"I told her to wait for me at her apartment until I got back."

The gun prodded me. "Come on. Let's see Ogundu."

"But he made me promise to come alone—"

"We'll surprise him, then. March."

I marched. I marched through the area-way

with the night wind in my face and the gun in
my back. When we got to the car, he put the
gun in his pocket, but his hand was never far
away.

The Lincoln roared. It was late, there was no
traffic on the street. We rode in darkness and
in silence, and then we came to a place of
darkness and silence. The Temple of the Living
Flame stood bleak and black.

We raced each other up the steps. I couldn't
see anything in the shroud of shadows. I might
have lit a match, but I didn't want to light a
match.

Weatherbee banged on the door. There was
no response. No light showed from within, no
footsteps sounded. The echoes of his pounding
mingled with the whispers of the wind.

I thought of another evening, when I'd stood
at Ricardi's door and vainly sought admit-
tance. I gazed around. No French windows
here.

"Maybe there's a rear entrance," Weatherbee
said. "Let's find out."

We descended the steps, found a narrow
walk between the Temple and the building
next to it. "You go first," he told me.

I started walking and he followed, gun out
now. I groped along, then rounded a corner of
the narrow passageway.

There was a back door. I pushed against it,
turning the knob. The door eased open.

"Come on," I whispered. "It's all right."

I blinked back into the darkness, waiting for him to come around the corner.

Then he did.

Weatherbee came around the corner very slowly. His hand clutched at the wall, and slid away as he fell.

"Weatherbee!"

I bent over the dim outlines of the figure sprawled there on the walk. I reached out and touched his face. It was cold. My fingers moved to his neck, came away wet and sticky in the darkness.

Then, as I straightened up, I caught the dull gleam in the shadows of the passageway. It was flashing towards me, toward my own throat—

I jerked back around the corner, yanking at the door, hurling myself forward.

Stumbling and gasping, I went over the threshold, then turned and slammed the door shut. I heard the lock click and catch.

This must be the basement entry to the Temple. I looked for a light-switch, then decided not to risk it. For I could hear the sound of the doorknob rattling outside. Then came a panting, the sound of furious blows against the wooden frame.

Turning, I groped along the corridor until my feet found the base of the stairway. Good. Anything was good that could take me away from that door, fast. These steps must lead up to the back hall, where Ogundu's office was located.

I rose through the darkness, reached a hall. I'd guessed right. A crack of light showed from under a door down the corridor. This was Ogundu's office and I prayed he'd be waiting for me.

I opened the door, and he was. He sat there smiling up at me calmly and quietly.

"Phil—thank God you're here!"

I whirled, shutting the door behind me. She'd been flattened against the wall, behind it. Now she came into my arms.

"Diana, what's the matter?"

She couldn't answer; she could only point.

I broke free and walked over to the smiling Negro. I moved around his chair and now I could see the back of his head—or what was left of it.

Ogundu had no reason to smile.

"What happened?" I muttered.

Diana shook her head. Her eyes avoided mine. I followed their stare to her hand; her right hand, holding the big .38.

We both looked at it for a long moment, and then she spoke. Her voice was only a whisper, but it filled the room, and its echo never died away.

"Yes, Phil. I killed him."

17

I TOOK THE GUN and laid it on the desk. "His?" I murmured.

Diana nodded. "He had it ready."

"Ready for what?"

"For you." She came to me. "Don't you see? I was right—it *was* supposed to be a trap."

I lifted her chin. "What happened? From the beginning."

"I came here after I left your place. I was afraid to go to the apartment and wait. I *had* to know."

"You should have waited. Or phoned the police instead."

"I can't help it, it's done now. Phil, don't torment me, isn't it bad enough to realize what I've gotten into without"—she began to sob. I held her close. In a moment she was able to go on.

"I used my own key and walked in. Ogundu must have gotten an awful scare, but he didn't show it. He just asked what I was doing here. So I told him I'd come because of you—you'd been delayed. And I wanted the information he'd promised."

"Did he tell you?"

Diana shook her head. "He said he wouldn't give it to anyone but you. You were the one who deserved to know. I asked him what he meant by that, and he wouldn't answer—just told me to go away. I said I wasn't going until I found out about all this.

"Then he looked at me and he said, 'You really mean that, don't you?' And he smiled and looked down at the floor and I saw the kerosene drum standing there."

Diana paused, and now I looked down. There *was* a kerosene drum, standing amidst a litter of papers. Something started to crawl along my spine. Diana's words only made it crawl faster.

" 'That's right,' he said. 'I was going to tell him the truth.' He pulled out the gun, then, and pointed it at me, and all the while he kept talking, telling me what he'd planned. He was waiting for you to come so he could kill you. Then he'd start the fire and phone the police— say he caught you, and killed you in self-defense. That would give the police a solution and put him in the clear. He hated you, Phil, because of your investigation. I guess he thought he could get rid of all the cults in town until you came along.

"But now, since you hadn't arrived, he was still going through with his plan. With me for a victim, instead." Diana closed her eyes. "He started to raise the gun—I made a grab for his wrist, twisted his arm around. Then the gun went off and he fell back into the chair.

"After that, I just stood there for a long time. I don't know how long. The next thing I remember is hearing footsteps outside in the hall. I got behind the door and you came in."

"That's all?" I asked.

She nodded.

"There'll be some tough sledding," I told her. "The police will ask a lot more questions."

Diana opened her eyes, wide. "You aren't going to call them?"

I nodded. "What else can I do?"

"Phil!" She stared up at me. "Phil, don't—"

"Suppose you tell me the truth, then. Suppose you tell me how you could have twisted Ogundu's wrist so the gun would shoot him through the back of the head?"

"He must have turned away—yes, I remember now, he broke loose for a second—"

She was pale and wide-eyed and the words were coming too fast. And I could feel myself slowly growing sick inside. Sick and cold. Somebody I had loved had died once. And now somebody I loved was dying again.

"Stop it, Diana! He was sitting in that chair

when you killed him. He wasn't struggling. He didn't know you were coming up behind him, ready to blow his brains out—"

She came closer and put her hands on my shoulders.

"Darling—you don't know what you're talking about—"

"Yes I do. I'm beginning to know a lot of things." I caught hold of the collar of her blouse. "You came here to kill Ogundu. Because the little white-faced man had told him you started the fires."

"No! That's impossible, you know yourself, the first time I was with you—"

"You left before one, and you went back to the Brotherhood tabernacle instead of going home. When you furnished an alibi for me to Dalton, you were also furnishing an alibi for yourself. Everything worked out fine, didn't it?"

Her mouth formed words, but none came.

"But there was one thing you hadn't counted on," I said. "The little guy must have seen you. And I suppose he started following you. He saw you the next day when you made a date with Ricardi. That's how you managed to kill him, isn't it? You promised to come to his house and you did—he wouldn't keep a pretty girl out of his bedroom. And that was his mistake. You knocked him out, set fire to his room."

I didn't have to think now, the words were falling into the place. The words—the deeds—

"The little guy knew. He found out you

worked here and he hung around, waiting for a chance to see Ogundu when he was alone. Tonight he did. And Ogundu called me.

"You got scared when you saw me visiting Ogundu and came over to find out if I'd learned anything. Then, when Ogundu phoned, you went into action. You killed him with his own gun and decided to carry out this crazy scheme of yours. Collected the paper, got the kerosene from the cellar—"

She froze. Frozen fire, in my arms.

"What are you going to do?"

I moved back. "What can I do? I'm going to call Dalton."

"No!"

She saw my hand go out, grabbed it. At the same time I reached for her blouse, tugged at it, jerking her to one side.

The blouse tore.

The blouse tore, down the front, and I saw what I didn't see in the darkness of the apartment, what I didn't see at the beach the time I started to open her dress and she ran away.

I saw what I'd seen on the curtain upstairs, what she'd told me about when she spoke of the Temple deacons and their ceremonies.

It was burned in her chest, burned red and deep above the breasts, burned in the whiteness of her flesh, just as it must be burned into the blackness of her brain.

I saw the brand of the Phoenix.

I stared at it, and that was my mistake. I

should have been staring at her hand, the hand that grabbed the gun from the desk, raised it, and brought the butt crashing down against my skull.

I went out, cold.

18

IT WASN'T cold any more.

It was warm and wet. Not sticky, like the blood that ran down the back of my scalp. This was a creeping wetness, flowing all over me. I could feel it plainly, just as I could feel the tightness in my wrists when she tied my hands behind my back. I was still lying on the floor, but I was wet.

I opened my eyes. She was standing over me, smiling. Smiling, and pouring kerosene.

"Awake?" she said. "Good. I'm glad. I wanted you to be awake. So you could see."

"See? I don't want to see anything. Diana, let me up—"

"No. You stay there. Stay there and watch. You wanted to find out what it's like, didn't you? You wanted to know. Now I'll show you."

The fumes rose, choking me. I twisted my wrists. She'd tied them with twine from the desk; tied them very tightly.

"Don't bother," she told me. "It's no use." She walked over to the heap of papers and dumped the rest of the kerosene on the litter.

"There. That ought to be enough, don't you think?" She giggled. "I suppose you think I'm being very naughty." Something had happened to her voice. If my eyes were closed, I'd have sworn it was a little girl speaking.

But my eyes weren't closed. They were open, and I could see her—see her standing there, a full-grown woman, with her coppery hair hanging down over bare shoulders, and the livid brand blazing between her breasts.

"Mama said I was naughty. When I made the fire in the basement she caught me and gave me a spanking."

I tried to get my legs up. She came over and knelt beside me. "Mustn't move," she murmured. "Mustn't be naughty." She giggled again and hit me with the gun. The side of my head went numb.

"Lie still, now. Lie still and watch. You want to see everything, don't you? How it starts?"

"Diana," I groaned. "For God's sake—"

"Yes, for God's sake. You *do* understand, don't you? He wants me to destroy the altars of abomination, to cleanse the earth of those who bow down to graven images, and the unrighteous, those who sin against the flesh and the spirit—" She was kneeling now, kneeling beside the pile of papers. There was a matchcarton in her hand.

Abruptly, her tone altered again. The child was gone, the fanatic was gone. Her voice was normal, intimately vibrant. "Oh, Phil, isn't it exciting? Wait and see. You can't imagine how lovely it is, how it makes you feel. It's like the way you must feel when you hold me. Only this is a clean feeling, it's pure and good, not like that other. No. Not the way *you* feel at all."

"Diana, stop it!"

"I'm going to stop it. I'm going to stop you. You, and all the rest of them, vessels of lust. This is what you want, isn't it? You and my mother and her men—this is all you think about!"

She crouched there, trembling. The matches fell from her fingers and her hands tore at the front of her blouse, ripping it all the way down.

"Look, then! Your hands are tied. You can't touch me. Nobody can touch me. See the brand? God told me to do that. Ogundu didn't know about the brand. God made me do it, to protect myself from evil. He sent me here to burn away all sin. To burn away all sinners."

She picked up the matches. I watched her strike a light. The paper kindled, flared.

"We won't need this now." She rose, switched

off the light. The flames licked and spread, sent shadows flickering across the wall.

"You can see, can't you?" she whispered. "You can watch it spread, now. Spread, and grow. I'm going to watch, too. I always run away, but this time I'll stay and watch. I want to see it burn."

The paper was blazing. It was red and blue, and now the drapes were red and blue, too, and I could feel the heat. The fire began to race across the floor toward me.

She stood against the wall and laughed. I rolled over, trying to get back into the far corner. The fire followed, creeping and eating and creeping again.

"Yes," she said. "I want to see it burn. I want to see you burn. The way that girl burned, the one you told me about. She was evil and so are you. I'm going to watch God's punishment. It's in the Bible, you know. How the wicked are cast into the flames. Don't you feel it yet, Phil? You will. In just a minute now. Yes!"

I wedged myself into the corner, trying to curl around the base of the desk. The fire flowed across the floor like a living lake, rising in a wave.

Diana began to gasp, but her eyes ever wavered. I could see the reflection of the flames pinpointed in her pupils.

"Burn! I want to see you burn! I want to see everything, Mama wouldn't let me see, she said it was wicked, but Mama's dead now. God killed her, He kills the wicked, and He told me I could see—"

It was horrible to hear the voice change, but watching her was even worse. The features formed and altered like a waxen mask melting in the heat of the flames; I saw Diana, I saw a child, I saw a woman in ecstasy. This was it, this was the pyromaniac, the method and the madness that needs no motive, the firebug—

I heard her scream.

The blaze was bright and I could see everything. I jerked my head back, staring above the sheet of flame.

Diana stood against the wall, near the door. The door was open, now, and somebody stood on the threshold, then moved forward into the light.

I saw the face, the white face that now shone red in the reflected glare.

But he didn't see me. He stared at the girl. "You," he said. "You burned the tabernacle. I saw you. I warned Ogundu tonight, but then I waited because I knew you'd come."

She crouched there, edging toward the door.

"Witch!" he shouted.

Suddenly she turned and darted out the doorway. He moved to block her path, then stepped aside. As she passed him, his arm rose and fell. I heard him shout again, and for a moment the words didn't register. It sounded like Biblical quotation—"Thou shalt not suffer a witch to live."

Then I understood why. I understood, when

Diana fell forward with the long knife driven deep between her shoulders.

The witch was dead . . .

I tried to get up and almost made it. The desk toppled with a crash, and I came down on top of it. It was like a little island in that sea of flame, and now the flame was rising all around, and the smoke was coming up to stifle me.

From far away I heard sounds, shouts, shots. It seemed to me that I saw the little man fall, but then the flames came up and I was falling too.

I began to burn.

19

IT WAS three days before they let me sit up. Even though the burns were all first-degree, I had on too many bandages for comfort.

When Dalton came to see me, I couldn't talk at all. Schwarm visited me the fourth day, and it was a little better.

"You'll be all right," he said. "Another week here, and then a rest. You're lucky they pulled you off that desk in time. If Clark hadn't thought to wrap his coat around you and smother the flames—"

"Never mind about Clark," I said. "What about the little guy? Did you find out his name?"

"Of course. It's John Schoober. We traced his record, too. Typical paranoid—"

"Why?" I muttered. "Because he thought Diana was a witch? I think so, too. Maybe you head-shrinkers have something to learn from the oldtimers. The ones who used to explain insanity in terms of demonic possession."

Schwarm smiled.

I asked questions, then, and pieced things together. It was the little guy who'd jumped Weatherbee in the passage, of course. He hadn't lied about tipping off Ogundu and then waiting around; when he saw us he got scared and gave Weatherbee a knife-wound in the throat.

After I locked the back door on him, he broke through a cellar window and came upstairs. He waited outside the door for a long while— almost too long, as far as I was concerned— until he got up enough courage to face the witch.

Meanwhile some kid came along and happened to notice Weatherbee lying in the passageway. He called a squad car, and the squad got there just about the time the fire became visible from outside the Temple.

That's when they broke down the front door and caught the little guy making his break for it. And Sergeant Clark came in on the double and pulled me out of the blaze.

Schwarm told me all about it now. He said they'd even dug up the dope on Diana Rideaux. He asked me to tell him what had happened, and I did my best.

"Exactly," he said, when I finished. "It all

fits in. The hatred of the mother. God as the father-image, idealized. Men as the actual father—feared and hated, fit only for destruction.

"The sexual pattern's there, too. Frigid but promiscuous. With fire as the symbol, fire that destroys passion and the male who can provoke it; fire that at the time purifies and preserves. It makes sense."

"The hell it does," I said. "She was a witch."

I told him about the earlier part of the evening, in my apartment—and then I told him about Margery, and my dreams.

"Well, at least you have one thing to be thankful for, Phil," he said. "You won't be getting those dreams any more."

"That's right," I answered.

Schwarm told the truth. I've never dreamed about Margery since then.

But there's a new dream now, a new dream to take its place. I get it whenever I go to sleep without enough in me to knock me cold.

I know it's only a dream, but that doesn't help me. I keep getting hotter and hotter, and I can feel the warmth on my face, and then I look up and see that *other* face. I see Diana's face in the flames, see her scream.

Then I wake up and reach for a cigarette, but I don't light it. I lay there trembling for a long time, wanting to smoke but not daring to. Because where there's smoke, there's fire.

And I'm afraid of fire.

At least, I always *have* been. God knows, I've

got reason enough to be afraid, and these dreams only make it worse.

But lately I've been doing a little thinking. Schwarm would say that the only way to conquer a phobia is to make yourself face it. And there's another way of putting it, too.

You've got to fight fire with fire. . .

Not that I'd actually *do* anything, understand. But I've been wondering. Suppose I could make myself get *used* to fire? So that I wouldn't be afraid of it?

I don't mean arson, incendiarism. I certainly wouldn't want to hurt anybody—not anybody who hadn't hurt me. But if I just experimented to see what it feels like, maybe down in the basement where nobody would know about it; that would be all right. I mean, I could keep water handy, put it out before anything really got started.

My idea is that I'm not actually afraid of the fire itself. Just the things that have happened to me in connection with fire.

Fire. It isn't something to be afraid of. Not if you can control it. That's the big secret, the way I see it. To *control* fire. Because when you control fire you control everything. Fire is life and it's death, too, and that's why it's so fascinating to watch it. To see it live and burn.

Maybe if I try an experiment or two, the dreams will go away. No harm in that; I'm going to be very careful. And if it helps me get rid of the dreams, that's all I want.

I suppose that's the real reason I've gone to

the trouble of writing everything down this way. So that people will understand that I know what I'm doing, why I'm doing it. And there won't be any foolish talk about firebugs.

Because it makes sense, doesn't it? It's not as if I didn't know the difference between the dreams and reality. If you're logical, you can always tell the difference. You live and learn. Live and burn.

Sometimes, lately, that phrase pops into my head when I least expect it. Like a voice. But it *isn't* a voice. You see, I know that. I know the difference between dreams and reality. And I'm just going to use reality to fight the dreams.

Maybe tonight—

THE BEST IN HORROR

RAMSEY CAMPBELL